DEATH RAISER

BOOKS BY J. C. MCKENZIE

Dark Legacy

Embrace the Flame

The Carus Series

Shift Happens

Beast Coast

Carpe Demon

Shift Work

Beast of All

Obsidian Flame

Dangerous Dreams

Dangerous Liaisons

Dangerous Decisions

That Old Black Magic

The Good Griffin

Standalones

Immortal Throne (with Harper A. Brooks)

Call of the Deep (The Shucker's Booktique)

Stormbound (Be My Love)

DEATH RAISER

J. C. McKenzie

COPYRIGHT INFORMATION

Death Raiser

Contact Information: jcmckenzie@jcmckenzie.ca

Cover Art: Tricia Beninato

Character Art: Kalynne_Art

Publishing History:

First JCM Publications Edition, 2023

ISBN: 978-1-990143-26-7 (print)

ISBN: 978-1-990143-27-4 (ebook)

To BookTok
for loving how Kang's gaze darkens
when he spots Lark in leather and heels.

You're entering the creative domain of a Canadian author. There will be a combination of British and American spellings, a combination of measurement systems, and maybe even a little French thrown in to spice things up. You've been warned...

This book contains explicit language, ghosts, spirits, souls, skeletons, bones, violence, blood magic, necromancy and animal sacrifices (off-the-page as much as possible).

Please read with care.

"Bones for bones,

blood for blood,

magic for magic.

Sacrifices are the life force of

death."

~ The Book of Life

Lark Morgan's
Rules to Necromancy

1. ~~Never use your own blood~~

2. ~~Never meet the Lord of the Veil~~

3. Never run into a barghest

4. Never reveal your lineage

5. Never take more than you need

R ed and blue lights flashed as I ducked under the yellow crime scene tape. The moon shone brightly overhead, illuminating evergreen trees that stood tall over the commotion at the path's entrance. Gravel crunched under the police officers' boots, people spoke in low, hushed voices, and an owl hooted in the distance as if trying to join the conversation.

Still summer, the air lacked the usual bite it held during the other nine months of the year. Crickets and katydids boisterously sang with each other, adding a loud hum as a backdrop to the morbid crime scene.

For a temperate rainforest, we hadn't seen a lot of rain in the Greater Victoria Area and the forest floor showed the impact with its dry grass and dead moss. The smell of baked pine needles, dirt, and sun-ripened blackberries surrounded me.

I approached the officer standing nearby with a clipboard and flashed my identification. "Lark Morgan to see Detectives Kang and Jacobs."

The officer nodded and held out the clipboard for me to sign in. His nametag read, "Shaw."

"Where's Rodriguez?" I asked.

The female officer was usually the one I checked in with. Her or Daniels. I didn't know this one.

Officer Shaw shrugged. "Don't know. Don't care."

I frowned and unclipped the pen to write down my details. The night hummed with death energy and called to the necromancer magic screaming in my veins. I handed back the clipboard and after a silent wave to Officer Shaw, walked down the marked path into the wooded area of the park. Worn for ease of cleaning blood spatter, not comfort, my leather vest and pants creaked with each step. I'd been tempted to throw on a pair of heels, just to see Kang's reaction, but as much as I would enjoy that, I wouldn't enjoy a broken ankle. My outfit was already impractical for the summer heat.

At least it was nighttime.

Though necromancers worked openly in society, we preferred to work in the cloak of darkness to avoid judgemental drabs. Besides, death magic was always stronger at night when the barrier between the living realm and the veil grew thinner.

Tonight, the power held an extra punch. With my experience working for Raisers, a registered necromancer-for-hire agency, I raised the dead almost every night. I'd become used to the nuances in energy. This was not a fresh death, but detectives Connor Kang and Oliver Jacobs felt the crime scene merited calling in a necromancer.

I'd worked for the Victoria Police Department for the last six years as a consultant. I would've preferred to be a member of the force and leave my job at Raisers, but the VicPD had a human-only hiring policy.

Technically, I was human, I just had a little extra spice in my blood.

The police department didn't see things that way, though. When they specified "human only," what they really meant was humans without any supernatural abilities—drabs. They were too good to hire a necromancer as a unionized staff member, but not good enough to not need one.

I sighed and pushed a branch out of my way.

Luckily, Kang and Jacobs didn't echo the sentiments of their agency. Probably because Kang wasn't exactly human, either.

Stepping off the path, I found Detective Kang right away. Despite wearing jeans and a light cotton, short-sleeved Henley, no one would mistake Kang as a civilian.

"About fucking time," Kang grumbled.

If Kang ever stopped greeting me with at least one swear word, I'd keel over from shock.

Around six foot three inches with a muscular

build, Kang didn't need the surly expression to make an impression, but that didn't stop him from always looking at people like they were going to be the final straw that finally made him lose his shit. He looked at me that way right now.

Hell, he always looked at me like that.

Kang had black hair, dark eyes, and chiselled cheekbones I could slice lemons on. A long scratch down his face appeared to be in the latter stages of healing, a visual reminder of how sideways our previous case had gone, but otherwise his skin was flawless. Despite working with him for more than half a decade, he appeared no older than the day we met.

The man could be fifty, and I wouldn't be able to tell.

"How old are you?" I blurted out.

Kang straightened, his dark eyebrows slashing downward. He hesitated before answering. "Thirty-four. Why?"

"Just checking," I muttered and approached the section of the crime scene where someone had draped a blanket over the victim's remains. Death magic pulsed from beneath the sheet.

Detective Jacobs stood off to the side speaking with one of the crime scene technicians. He looked over when I spoke. "Don't let Kang's grizzly behaviour fool you," Jacobs called out. "He missed you."

I turned to Kang and blew him a kiss. "I missed you, too."

Kang scowled harder and somehow the severe expression looked good on him.

I'd seen the detective a week ago. He didn't miss me for a second, though he had sent flowers to my office—a beautiful bouquet of red roses. I'd have to ask him about the rose I'd found outside my apartment this morning, but now wasn't the time.

"What about me?" Jacobs yelled out.

"I always miss you, Jacobs," I shot over my shoulder at the other detective.

Kang rolled his eyes and let out a long, suffering breath.

If Kang reminded me of sultry nights filled with wicked promises, Jacobs was all sunshine and daisies. He had the boy next door charm and a wide endearing smile that could get a serial killer acquitted of murder charges. He'd been in the sun for too long recently and his usually fair skin had a notable red tinge to it. His blond hair had lightened to an almost white colour, and he looked like he should be wearing a Hawaiian shirt, board shorts and a straw hat, walking around a tropical resort with a drink in his hand and zinc paste on his nose.

Instead, he wore a T-shirt and fitted jeans.

"You asked my age because you were *just checking*?" Kang repeated my earlier comment and drew my attention away from his partner. "Just checking for what?" Kang still frowned as if trying to solve one of those Rubik's cubes.

I sighed. He'd never drop this, so I may as well come clean. "I had this random thought about how I can't tell how old you are, and you could very well be fifty."

A slow smile spread across Kang's face, and he leaned toward me. "A random thought?"

"Yep. Totally." I turned toward the body. "What do we have here?"

"What we have here is a classic, yet mediocre, deflection tactic, Morgan. And I'm not going to allow it," Kang said, his deep voice rumbling. "Why were you thinking about my face?"

"Hard not to when you're scowling at me." He was on to me. I'd thought about his face more often than I'd like. Though I was thirty-one years old, something about this man made my heart flutter and rational thought flee my brain, making me feel and act like a preteen with my first crush.

If anyone managed to get a sneak peek into my brain, I'd die of mortification.

"As much as I adore watching you turn this particularly lovely shade of red, we have a job to do." Kang chuckled and stepped forward to nod at the covered body. "Her name is Amy Steele. She reported missing six months ago, and from preliminary inspection, it appears she's been here for most of that time."

Yikes. This would not be a pleasant body to view. "Scavengers?"

"Many."

"Decomp?"

"Bad."

I couldn't smell anything. Small miracles. Though if she'd been out in the elements for six months, which included the summer months, there wouldn't be much left on her bones, anyway.

"Who found her?" I asked. It made no difference for death raising, but curiosity happened to be one of my biggest vices.

"Dog walker."

"I'm never getting a dog," I muttered.

"Why not?" Kang's eyebrows shot up and he waved at the crime scene. "It's not like stumbling upon a dead body would scare you. It wouldn't even catch you by surprise. You're probably one of the best people to randomly stumble upon a body. I mean, other than a cop."

"Uh...thanks?"

"Do you not like dogs?" Kang asked. "I thought you loved animals."

"I *do* love animals, Kang." I turned to glance at the covered body. I didn't want Kang to see the hurt on my face. I might love all animals. Hell, I'd swim with piranhas if they wouldn't pick my bones clean. And most animals loved me back—something about my death magic calmed them—but for some reason, dogs never seemed to like me.

"Any other insight the coroner was willing to give?" I asked.

A forensic pathologist would do an autopsy at a later date and the findings would be communicated in the official report issued by the B.C. Coroners Service, but coroners often gave initial findings so detectives could start their investigations.

Kang studied my face and frowned. Yeah, I probably hadn't fooled him at all with my latest deflection attempt.

"From the damage to the portion of the skull recovered at the scene, the victim sustained a fatal gunshot wound to the head, though the coroner couldn't confirm that was the actual cause of death without further analysis," Kang finally answered. Apparently, he didn't plan to call me out for trying to avoid another question. "He couldn't say much more than that. The body was too decomposed. We can't even officially rule this is a homicide, yet."

"What makes you think it's Amy Steele?"

"Identification found in her pocket." He looked into the forest for a few moments before speaking again. "The timing of the missing persons report matches the level of decay. The autopsy will hopefully confirm the ID by matching dental records."

I nodded and stepped forward. "Do you have a chicken?"

Raising the dead required power, bones, and blood. A chicken was enough for what I needed to accomplish.

Technically, I could offer my own blood as the

sacrifice, but that would send me to the veil—the realm where souls lingered after death. In order to use my own blood safely, I needed an anchor as a way to avoid getting stuck in the veil. I'd exchanged blood with the Master Vampire of Victoria for this exact reason, but the bond grew weaker each day and I didn't want to rely on Gregor any more than I already did.

Even with a way back to the living realm, though, travelling to the veil held more danger than angry souls and getting stuck. Leviathan, Lord of the Veil, lurked in his castle waiting to pounce for reasons still unknown to me, and there were also barghests to contend with—demonic guard dogs who hated necromancers. I hadn't met one of those yet, and I wasn't exactly in a rush to scratch that item off my necromancer bucket list. Going to the veil was risky, if not borderline suicidal.

Thankfully, I didn't have to go to the veil to raise a spirit. So, I didn't need to use my own blood as a sacrifice in the foreseeable future, and a chicken would suffice.

To ensure their deaths weren't meaningless or solely for raising the dead, a local butcher took my sacrificed poultry chickens and sold them to families in need at a reduced rate. I still hated this part of my job, though. I hadn't lied to Kang. I loved animals. Taking their lives killed something inside me each time.

"Jacobs brought a chicken. He's been bitching

about how it messed up the back of his vehicle again," Kang said.

"He needs to get a crate," I said.

"That's what I keep telling him."

We shared a smile.

I crouched by the edge of the blanket and lifted the corner. The lingering smell of rot still clinging to the bones rushed out and I quickly dropped the heavy cloth.

"It's not pleasant," Jacobs approached with a chicken cradled under his arm.

"Thanks for the heads up," I said, though his warning was a little too late.

Jacobs winced and handed the chicken to me. After the sacrifice, he'd take the chicken and bag it for me while I spoke to the spirit. We had a pretty good routine. I raised the dead. Jacobs assisted and Kang stood nearby with a sour expression plastered to his handsome face. The important part was not to drop the chicken. If I did, the butcher couldn't use it, and I'd get yelled at for contaminating the crime scene.

"Is the body cleared for me to handle?" I asked.

"Yes." Kang stood close to the body. "Do you need to handle it?"

"Hopefully not." I had a lot of power. If the death was fresh, I didn't even need the blood to touch the bones to raise the spirit. I only had to be close to the body. The older the remains, however, the more contact I needed to forge a connection. Physically touching the bones and spilling blood on the bones created the strongest bond. Hopefully, I only had to resort to the latter. I preferred to avoid touching the remains.

Kang nodded and knelt to grab the corner of the cloth. "Let me know when you're ready."

I pulled a knife from my pocket and unfolded the blade in a well-practiced move. I didn't often work on bodies with a lot of decomposition because Kang and Jacobs usually got fresher crime scenes. How much worse could this one be? "Ready as I'll ever be."

Kang grimaced and pulled back the sheet.

My brain misfired, trying to process the mangled remains in front of me. How could this possibly have been a human?

Stomach acid bubbled up my throat and my gut twisted. I swallowed nausea down and took a deep breath.

And instantly regretted it.

"Are you okay?" Kang asked.

I swallowed again and contemplated running over to the bush to throw up. "Never better."

Kang narrowed his eyes and pressed his lips together.

No fooling him. I looked over at Jacobs. "Ready?"

"Always."

I cut the chicken's throat quickly and let the blood drip onto the exposed femur jutting out from the tangled mass of limbs. Without looking, I handed the chicken to Jacobs, embraced the death magic around me and pushed the power through the bones. I mumbled an incantation and called out to the deceased. "Amy Steele."

The spirit would still come even if I used the wrong name, but it made the pull stronger.

Energy surged up and answered my call. The death magic hung dark and sticky around me. A shaking spectre formed over the blood-drenched bones and wailed.

Kang stiffened beside me. Whatever he was, he could see and hear spirits without me having to force them into reanimating their corpses. I'd also found out on our last case together he could identify the unique smell of souls. Kang was full of surprises but to onlookers he pretended to be like everyone else.

Everyone "normal."

Drab.

We'd worked together for six years—six long, frustrating years—and I had no inkling Kang wasn't a drab until our last case together when he'd reacted to an invisible spirit's wailing. I didn't know what kind of glamy he was, but I planned to find out. Discreetly, of course.

Kang might be a grumpy asshole who said some mean things to me, but I'd keep his secret. I didn't want him to lose his job. He was good at what he did—ruthlessly hunting down murderers and making sure they received maximum sentencing for their crimes.

Kang excelled in his role, and I did, too.

"Amy?" I called out. "Amy is that you?"

The spirit continued to shake and wail.

"Amy. My name is Lark Morgan. I'm a necromancer consultant with the Victoria Police Department. We found your remains and want to know what happened. Can you answer some questions? We need to know who did this to you."

Amy stopped wailing. Shaking her head back and forth, her phantom hair covered her pale face. She wrapped her arms around her chest and swayed side to side. The T-shirt, jeans and sneakers she wore were covered with dirt, and her exposed arms were lined with scratches.

I exchanged a look with Kang.

"What's the problem?" Jacobs asked.

"The spirit is too distraught to speak," I answered, knowing Kang couldn't. Wouldn't.

"Will she calm down given time?" Jacobs asked.

"Maybe. But it's already been about six months if you think the body was dumped here shortly after she went missing. Her death isn't fresh. It's draining to hold a spirit for a long time, though, and there's also a risk of her soul becoming volatile and escaping my control. I'd rather set her free."

We'd recently dealt with an angry spectre who possessed the partners of cheating women to slaughter them. That hadn't been a fun case and the necromancer who'd raised the spirit was still at large.

Whomever they were, they had a lot to answer for.

The spirit had gone on a murdering spree and even possessed Kang for a few minutes before Kang kicked the spirit from his mind. But the spirit had taken root long enough for me to find out Kang had feelings for me and long enough for the spirit to try to kill me using Kang's anger, frustration, and physical strength. I survived by escaping to the veil and taking the spirit with me.

After the whole I-got-possessed-and-tried-to-kill-you fiasco, Kang had sent flowers to my work. This time the bouquet of roses had a card with an apology note for almost strangling me.

My hand drifted to my neck involuntarily. Under the chain of my necklace, the bruises from the attack had mostly healed, leaving a slight yellow discolouration on my fair skin.

Kang had nothing to be sorry for except not asking me out and leaving me confused as fuck.

"Yeah," Jacob said. "We don't want another volatile spirit rampaging around Victoria."

Kang shuddered and looked away.

Amy wailed again, opening her mouth wide to howl at the sky.

"She doesn't have a tongue," I whispered.

"What?" Jacobs and Kang turned toward me in unison.

"Someone cut out her tongue." My stomach twisted

in a knot. I glanced down at her physical remains. Due to the level of decomposition and the impact of scavengers on her body, the coroner wouldn't have picked up this detail—at least not here at the crime scene. A full autopsy might've revealed the information, but it was doubtful. "Amy...can you give us any hint to who did this?"

Amy continued to wail. She turned to run away, but my magic held her in place. The knot in my stomach tightened. This wasn't right. I shouldn't be holding her. Amy needed to find peace. She deserved it.

The spirit stopped running, and the wailing stopped. She swayed back and forth some more, rubbing her arms.

"Who are you running from Amy?" I asked.

She shook her head, back and forth.

"Who did this to you?"

Amy finally looked up, her hair falling to the side to reveal white eyes that had glazed over. Her cheeks were hollowed out as if starved before she died. She met my gaze and screamed.

I flinched and leaned away.

Amy kept screeching, the pitch high in the air and eardrum-shattering. Her death energy pulled at my control.

"Lark?" Kang shouted. "Let her go, Lark."

"Why are you yelling?" Jacobs whispered.

Wincing under the sheer volume of screams, I

gathered my magic and mumbled the incantation to banish Amy's spirit back to the veil.

The wailing stopped, fading away into the night, replaced with the low rumble of conversations and the crunch of boots on the path.

I blinked open my eyes. I had somehow ended up sprawled on the ground, halfway between kneeling and laying on my side.

Kang walked over to me and held out his hand. "Here."

I reached up and grabbed it, letting him haul me to my feet.

"Are you okay?" he asked for the second time since I arrived at the crime scene.

"I will be."

He didn't let go right away. Instead, he stayed still, only inches away and studied my face. His subtle cologne wrapped around me, and I tried desperately to ignore how good he smelled.

"Are you smelling me?" His lips quirked up at the corners.

I totally was. God, he smelled good. I shook my head and stepped back, pulling my hand from his warm grasp. "I see you're still delusional."

Kang smirked and turned to Jacobs. "Not sure where we can go from here. The lack of evidence surrounding the body suggests she was dumped shortly after death, but we'll have to wait until forensics finishes their investigation and issues their formal report."

Jacob sighed. "I guess we're going to have to canvas the area. See if anyone saw anything suspicious."

Kang grunted.

"Did she say anything useful?" Jacobs asked.

Kang opened his mouth to say something, but I stepped in. "Not really. She screamed and tried to run away. Her appearance was also very gaunt and she was covered in dirt and scratches. I suspect she had been starving prior to her death."

Kang nodded at me.

When Kang confirmed he wasn't quite the drab he presented himself to be, I'd asked him who else knew. Apparently, only his partner Jacobs. Nobody else suspected, or if they did, they wisely kept it to themselves. Hell, it took me six years to figure it out. We needed to keep this act up for all the other officers and forensic analysts milling around the edges of the crime scene or Kang would lose his job.

"That gives us something. The killer is smart enough to anticipate a necromancer and cut out the tongue," Jacobs said.

"Shouldn't everyone anticipate a necromancer?" I asked. "It's not like necromancers working for the police is new."

Jacobs scoffed. "You'd think, right? Not everyone is smart and not all police departments contract necromancers, so we gain a little insight into the killer's mind. This probably wasn't a crime of passion and probably not the killer's first victim. Personally, I prefer the messy, clueless ones," Jacob said before turning to Kang. "I need to ask the technician some stuff. You guys can finish up here. Catch you later, Morgan."

I nodded and lifted my hand in a half wave. "No offense, Jacobs, but hopefully, we don't see each other too soon."

"Hah! You'd die of boredom without us, Morgan." The detective turned away with a smirk and walked over to where a forensic technician waited, leaving me with the dead body and a grumpy cop.

Kang frowned at his partner before returning his attention to me. "Do you need a ride home?"

I straightened, not expecting that question. Usually, I got dismissed and had to find my own way back to my apartment.

"This spirit seemed to really affect you," Kang explained. "Maybe it's not such a good idea for you to head home on your own."

"I drove," I said. "I don't want to leave my car here."

"We can take your car and I'll get someone to pick me up or I'll catch a cab back," he said.

"You seem intent on giving me a ride."

He leaned in. "You have no idea."

I laughed and shook my head. "If I didn't know any better, I'd say you were worried about me."

Hell, if I didn't know any better, I'd say he was flirting, too.

Kang sighed and looked over his shoulder. The others were busy talking and processing the scene. "I just witnessed a spirit's wailing bring you to your knees, Lark. Let me take you home."

Kang rarely used my first name, but when he did, it made my knees weak and did funny things to my stomach.

I...I think I liked it.

Ugh.

I totally liked it.

Kang's determined expression told me I shouldn't bother arguing about the ride. If I truly pushed back, he'd respect my answer despite his feelings on the matter, but he was right. I wasn't okay and having someone else drive me was probably for the best.

"Fine," I relented.

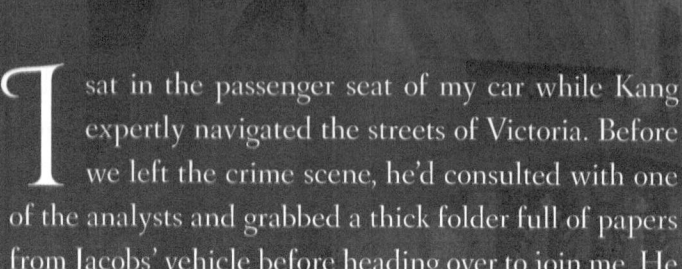

I sat in the passenger seat of my car while Kang expertly navigated the streets of Victoria. Before we left the crime scene, he'd consulted with one of the analysts and grabbed a thick folder full of papers from Jacobs' vehicle before heading over to join me. He dumped the folder in the backseat and held open the passenger door for me to get in.

It was almost sweet.

Oh hell, it was sweet.

And I had no idea how to process Kang taking care of me, so I remained speechless for the first half of the trip.

Kang didn't need directions. He'd dropped me off at the apartment building numerous times but even if he hadn't, he would've known my address. Kang was the type to investigate everyone in his life, in both a personal and professional capacity.

Part of me wanted him to keep driving around so I could avoid going home.

This morning, I'd found a single rose outside my apartment door. Technically, it could've been for my assassin brother Logan or his lawyer boyfriend Brandon, but something about the rose gave me chills. Why would anyone leave a flower outside our apartment door without a note?

Logan and Brandon swore they weren't fucking with me, which I took with a grain of salt, but if they didn't leave it, who did? The only other person who'd sent me flowers recently was Kang.

"Random question," I started. Kang really wasn't the type to sneak into an apartment building to leave a flower for a woman, he was too direct for cat and mouse games. But I had to ask. "Did you leave me a flower?"

"A flower?" Both his eyebrows shot up.

He didn't leave the rose.

"Uh, yeah. Someone left a rose without a note." I didn't dare say where or when. That would probably result in Kang calling the Emergency Response Team. I had no need for ERT to swarm my building—at least not until I knew for certain whether this was something serious or not. The rose hadn't been left inside my apartment, after all. Someone might've dropped it, and I was playing amateur flower detective for no reason.

"I sent a bouquet to your work a while ago, and

another bouquet more recently, but I have a feeling that's not what you're referring to." He pressed his lips together and remained silent while he turned onto another street. "I didn't leave you a rose, Lark."

His use of my first name again sent warmth flooding through my body.

"But now I'm worried about who did," Kang said.

"You don't need to worry." I was definitely worrying enough for the two of us.

"Are you dating someone? What happened to that Hudson guy?"

I froze at the name. Hudson Harrison and I had dated briefly until he tricked me and used me to hitch a ride to the veil. We were definitely not dating. Harrison probably wasn't even his real surname. "I'm not seeing anyone, Kang."

He shook his head. His grip on the wheel tightened.

"Are you okay?" I asked.

"I'm debating whether to pull over."

"And do what?"

He pressed his lips together. "I'm not sure."

"Lock me up? Shove me into a padded room? Chain me in your basement?"

He thought about it for an entire city block. "Those all sound reasonable."

"Kang..."

"It would only be until I found this rose-giving shit-head. I'd let you go after I knew you were safe."

"I can take care of myself, Kang."

"If you're in a situation where you have to take care of yourself, that's a problem."

"It's not a problem," I insisted. Yet.

He glanced at me, gaze narrow. Barely controlled rage simmered beneath the surface and the dark part of me wanted to reach out and stroke it, just to see what would happen. "Are you sure about that?"

"Yes," I said. "If that changes, I'll let you know."

"Promise?"

"Of course."

"Should I even be dropping you off at home alone? You have mysterious flowers showing up and you almost fainted at the crime scene today."

"First, there was only one rose, as in singular, and second, I really feel fine," I said. "I could've driven myself home."

He nodded, keeping his eyes on the road. His lips pressed together, and I could almost see the proverbial steam coming out of his ears. "I'd rather we not find out whether that was true while you're driving on the highway at night."

I sighed and dropped my head back on the headrest. "Thank you."

Kang nodded again and silence filled the car, not quite uncomfortable, but not quite comfortable, either. I had so much to say but didn't know where to start.

"How are you doing?" I finally asked.

"Fine. I've seen a bad decomp before," Kang said.

"That's not quite what I'm asking about." I played with the buttons on my jacket. "On our last case together, you were possessed by an angry spirit who tried to kill me. We haven't really talked since then."

He pressed his lips together and didn't respond.

I looked out the window and watched the street-lights fly by. He trusted me with knowing he had glamy abilities, although not what kind, why couldn't he trust me with his feelings? We hadn't spoken about the possession, and from Kang's reaction, we probably never would.

"It was the oddest thing," he said.

I jumped a little in my seat. He'd actually answered me. I held my breath and waited.

"I could feel the spirit slithering under my skin," he continued. "I could feel her anger, and then her frustration when she couldn't take over my mind right away."

"But she did."

Kang squeezed the steering wheel, making the plastic creak. "Eventually, yes. I wasn't strong enough."

I reached out and rested my hand on his forearm. He stiffened under my touch. "It's not your fault, Kang. You didn't do anything wrong. I don't blame you for anything that happened. You need to know that."

"I was getting her out of my head," he said. "I almost had her, but she would've choked you to death before I managed to remove her. If you hadn't wrenched her out of my body and taken her to the veil,

I would've killed you." He glanced over at me. His pained gaze dropped to the faded bruises on my neck, and he clenched his teeth together hard enough to make the muscles along his jawline pop out.

"But you didn't."

He swallowed and refocused on the road. "I didn't."

I removed my hand from his arm and went back to staring out the window.

"But you know what I realized?" he asked.

"What's that?"

"I want to take you out on a date."

Surprised laughter bubbled out of me. "It took getting possessed by a murderous spirit and nearly choking me to death to realize that?"

A smile tugged at his lips. "When you say it like that..."

"Seriously. I thought you would've figured that out after our dance."

During the last case, we ended up at a club where we danced together in order to blend in while we waited for the angry spirit to show up. I was still trying to recuperate from the experience. If Kang made love like he danced, I wouldn't survive the encounter.

I mean, not that I wanted to sleep with Kang.

Not really.

Okay, maybe.

Oh hell, I totally wanted to. I wanted to badly.

Apparently, I had a kink for grumpy detectives. Who knew?

Kang pulled into my parking spot and shoved it into park before turning to me. "I've known I wanted you for a long time, Lark."

I frowned. "Now I'm confused."

He sighed and popped off his seatbelt. "Dating is not a casual thing for me."

"That's funny. From what Jacobs says, I thought all you ever did was casual."

"Let me rephrase. Dating *you* will not be casual." His gaze flashed. "If you're not ready for something serious, you should tell me now."

I narrowed my eyes. What made me so special? Why did I get that distinction when other women didn't? And if he felt that way about me, why would he hesitate to ask me out? While I'd been dating since we met, I hadn't been in any serious relationships except with Ricky, and that ended disastrously. But the lack of a committed relationship wasn't from a lack of trying. I wanted a long term, loving connection with someone. Something like what Logan and Brandon had. I wanted that true love for me, too.

Not only was I ready for *something serious*, I'd actively searched for it for years. "Tell you now? Do you honestly think I wanted to flitter around from one awkward first date to another?"

"No."

"Then what the hell, Kang?"

If he knew I wanted something serious, and he wanted that with me, too, why did he wait years to ask me out?

He flinched. "That was a dick question. Every time I thought to ask you out, you ended up dating someone else."

"You should've said something, Kang."

"I wasn't sure you reciprocated my feelings, but more importantly, I don't believe in holding life-altering secrets from someone I'm in a relationship with," he said. "You only figured out I was a glamy last week."

Ah. There it was. One piece to the hot mess of Figuring-Out-Kang puzzle. "Would you have told me if I hadn't discovered the truth?"

"Maybe." He looked away. "If it was only my secret, yes."

More pieces fell into place. From our conversations over the years, I knew he had a sister nearby, and his parents lived in the city as well. That meant whatever Kang was, it had to be hereditary. If he got outed, his whole family would be, too. He had to keep the secret for them just as much as he did for himself, yet he didn't want to keep the truth from me, either.

Now, he didn't have to make that hard choice. I'd figured it out all on my own. Well...most of it.

"You haven't asked me what I am," he said.

I hadn't. That was considered a rude question within the glamy community. I didn't want to put him on the spot. He obviously hid his true nature for very good reasons. "I figured you'd either tell me when you were ready or you're hoping I'd figure it out with my superior intellect."

He chuckled and shook his head. "I guess it's a bit of both."

I popped off my seatbelt and turned to him expectantly.

He didn't elaborate.

"Thank you for the ride home." I held my hand out for the keys, he placed them in my palm and opened the door. I mirrored his actions, getting out of the car.

"Would you like to come upstairs while you wait for your ride?" I bit my lip to refrain from saying something more scandalous.

Kang paused, his lips quirking up at the corners. Something wicked flashed in his gaze and he leaned forward over the roof of my car to inhale deeply. He smiled, a slow, knowing smile that told me he knew exactly where my mind had wandered.

Instead of vaulting over the vehicle, though, he stayed safely on his side. "Thank you, but I don't trust myself to come upstairs."

"Why not?"

"You mentioned the possibility of tying you up and now my mind is going wild with possibilities. I won't respect your boundaries."

"That sounds...terrible." I lied. Now I was tempted to insist he escort me upstairs.

"Lark, I'll lock you up and start investigating the whole mysterious rose thing, and you'll never forgive me."

He was right, but not for the reasons he thought. "I wouldn't forgive you for choosing to spend my time tied up trying to solve a mystery," I said.

"Careful."

I ignored his warning. "I'm surprised you didn't accept my offer to do exactly that."

"I'm trying to be good."

"How's that working for you?"

"Not well."

"Are you mentally running through ways to sneak into my building to set up surveillance?"

He pursed his lips. "Maybe."

"Kang."

"Morgan."

"The flower thing is handled."

He grumbled and his dark gaze flashed with promise across the roof of the car.

"How will you get home?"

He blinked at me and pulled out his phone to check his messages. "I'll take a cab. Jacobs drove and he's still finishing up the scene."

I nodded and shifted my weight from foot to foot.

"You haven't answered my question," he said.

"I wasn't aware you asked one." I refrained from whistling or batting my eyelashes innocently. He hadn't asked me out, he only mentioned he wanted to.

Kang reached into the back of the car and picked up a thick file he'd placed there at the beginning of our trip. He walked around my car and closed the distance between us. Tucking the folder under his arm, he reached out to gently cup the side of my face. He stroked my cheek with his thumb and leaned in. "Will you let me take you out on a date?"

I'd probably let him do a hell of a lot more than that right now if he asked.

He didn't.

Instead, he studied my face again as if mesmerized by the tiny spattering of freckles across my nose and cheekbones. His gaze snagged on my healing bruises again and sucked in a quick breath.

"Yes," I whispered.

"I look forward to it." Kang leaned down and pressed a gentle kiss to my cheek. Taking a step back, he pulled the folder from under his arm and held it out toward me.

I used the key fob to lock the car doors before shoving the keys in my purse. I pointed at the thick folder. "What's this?"

"It's a copy of your father's missing persons case."

I stared down at the folder, not trusting my hands to touch it yet. My heart rate picked up and my scalp prickled. Dad went missing fifteen years ago and while I'd resigned myself to never learning his fate, I still clung to hope. "Why do you have it?"

"I've been working on the case for years, but I'm

sorry to say I'm no closer to discovering what happened to him than I was six years ago."

Six years ago.

He'd been working on this case, on the side, since he met me.

I swallowed, my mouth dry, my heart beating madly.

He'd looked into my father's disappearance after he'd saved my life. Kang didn't hate me at all. He... cared...for me. And now I knew he also liked me and my entire understanding of the world around me was crashing down.

"I should've given you a copy sooner," he said.

I reached out and took the folder from him and hugged it to my chest. My eyes stung and I blinked rapidly to hold the tears back. "Thank you."

"I need you to know I would've given you the folder regardless of whether you agreed to go on a date with me."

I scoffed and shook my head. "I never doubted your honour, Kang."

He reached forward and trailed his finger along my neck and down my collar bone before hooking it around the gold chain of my necklace. With a gentle tug, he lifted the pendant. "You've worn this every time I've seen you since our first case together. Is it your father's?"

"In a way," I said. "He had one made for me and Logan to match the one he has. Had. My brother refuses to wear his, but he keeps it in a box on his dresser."

"But you wear yours."

I plucked the dangling pendant and tilted it so the nearby light glinted off the surface. Someone had meticulously engraved a griffin clutching and chomping down on a skull in the center of the circular pendant. The symbol for descendants of the Morcant bloodline.

"I'll never give up hope," I said.

Kang dropped his hand to his side. "Neither will I."

THREE

I mumbled the incantation to bring forth the spirit to the living realm. Johnny Wheeler's spirit had a light blue shine and a wispy appearance. He hovered over his remains and shook his head. His living wife stood a few feet behind me, waiting for her deceased husband to arrive. She had no idea he was already here. Drabs couldn't see spirits. Hell, most glamies couldn't, either.

The moon cast an eerie glow over the cemetery, creating long shadows over the hallowed ground and illuminating the gravestones that stood in the tidy rows.

"Get in your corpse, Johnny." I shoved more magic at him, but he kept his position and continued to shake his head.

Standing beside Johnny's wife, Peter Schmidt waited patiently. I worked with this lawyer regularly, though Peter usually covered estate law, not spousal closure requests.

Monica, the wife, shifted her feet. "He's...he's here?"

"Yes, but he's being a little ornery. Sometimes spirits don't wish to reanimate their corpses."

"Why not?"

"I had a soul describe it like getting into dirty, wet clothes." They needed extra motivation.

"Last chance," I warned Johnny.

He swayed back and forth over his coffin as if to mock me.

Fine.

I knelt down, touched one of the exposed bones from his decaying body and pushed my magic in.

Johnny squealed. My magic yanked his spirit into his body.

"There we go," I whispered. "Home sweet home."

Johnny flailed his arms.

Monica gasped.

I muttered another incantation to get him to obey my commands and keep control of him. The last thing anyone in Victoria needed was a zombie running loose. Their bites weren't infectious, they were just a nuisance.

Usually.

"Feel your body, Johnny. Reconnect with it and stand up," I ordered.

He scrambled to his feet and swayed, waiting for

his next command. A wind rustled through the nearby trees, unusually cold for this time of year.

I turned to allow Monica an unobstructed view of her deceased husband. She held her hand to her mouth as if it would somehow block the smell of decay or take away the intrusion of the resting spirit.

"Babe?" Monica dropped her hand and stepped forward "Is that you?"

"Monica?" His voice came out raspy. The larynx had already started to break down. "Why did you do this? You know how much I hated the idea of this."

If he hated it so much, he should've had the additional restrictions added to his will.

Monica hesitated and glanced at me. "Is he feeling pain?"

"Not at this moment, no. Reanimating is often disorienting, though."

"But he can?" she asked.

"Can what?"

"Feel pain?"

I shrugged. "To an extent."

Monica didn't wait for an explanation. She stepped forward, drew her arm back and punched Johnny in the face. His head snapped back and a bone cracked. Instead of sitting properly on his neck, his head now listed to one side.

I rocked back on my heels and exchanged a look with Peter. He grimaced and shrugged. The laws were a little gray when it came to violence against a reanimated corpse. Some people had tried to go after clients in the past for desecration of remains, but the courts had thrown out every case so far.

"Fuck, Monica. What was that for?" Johnny wailed.

"What was that for?" Monica screeched the question back, hitting the corpse over and over again. "No. You meant to ask *who* that was for."

I bit my lip.

"And so far, there's Beatrice, Becky, Sarah, Michelle and Tara."

Oh dear.

"Are there more?"

Johnny dropped his mouth open but didn't reply.

"How many?" Monica demanded. "How. Fucking. Many?"

"A few." He winced.

"Who?"

"I...I didn't know their names. At least not all of them. Their names didn't matter. It was always you. I loved you. I have always loved you more."

Did he seriously say that? What a backward compliment. If Monica wasn't already beating him to a pulp, I would've been tempted to take a stab at him.

"Why didn't you just leave me?" she asked. "If you wanted other women so badly, why not free yourself? Why not free me, if you loved me so much?"

"Because I love you and I love our son. I love our family."

"Did you think about your family while you were plowing through the entire catalogue of available, and not-so-available women of Victoria?" Monica asked.

Johnny flinched.

Monica took a deep breath and curled her hands into fists. "Are there any children I should know about? Is your estate going to be sued for child support?"

I frowned. Could the court even do that? A glance at Peter and his responding nod told me yes. Huh.

At least I knew why Peter was here. The possibility of additional heirs would make settling the estate trickier.

"No...no children."

"You're sure?"

"I had a vasectomy three years ago."

"You what?" Monica started to breathe heavily. Pain streaked across her expression.

Without asking, I knew, *just knew*, Johnny hadn't told his wife about the vasectomy. I'd just met Johnny, but so far, he seemed like a complete piece of shit.

"Did you need anything else from him?" I asked, Johnny might be stubborn, but he wasn't particularly strong. I could hold him for longer. If Monica needed closure, though, hopefully, this was enough. Spending even one more second with this piece of work was a waste of our time.

"No," Monica whispered. "I got what I needed."

I glanced at Peter again and he nodded. They had the confirmation they needed. With a deep breath, I withdrew my power. Normally, spirits were ready to race away to the veil.

Not Johnny.

After I detached his spirit from his body and his corpse crumpled back into the open coffin with a thud, Johnny's spirit remained.

The blue spectre hovered over the open grave, bobbing a couple of feet away from my face, eerily silent. I gathered my magic to banish him to the veil when he sped forward.

"What the—"

"He wants a word." Johnny latched onto me and used my magic to send us both hurtling to the land of the dead.

CHAPTER
FOUR

I slammed into the cold ground and death magic swirled around me so fast it threatened to steal the air from my lungs. I released Johnny's spirit and clambered to my feet. A breeze whipped my hair in every direction. There was always a constant wind in this place. Death magic flowed around me, and curious spirits whirled by, swirling like little tornadoes of energy trying to vie for my attention. An ethereal mist rolled over the barren, uneven ground.

Pain stabbed at my fingers as my nails grew into long, dark talons. I watched as they elongated. Would I ever find out why my body reacted to the veil this way?

"We meet again." A deep voice made me jump and spin around.

The Lord of the Veil stood a few feet away, his castle looming close behind him. The structure rose from rocky terrain with a long winding path leading to the wrought iron gate at its main entrance. Outside the gate, a row of skeletons hanging on spikes acted as a better deterrent than any alarm system or guard dog. The gothic castle screamed danger and death and yet my curiosity begged me to get inside and have a look.

Logan would love this place.

Instead of running away, I faced the owner of the castle. With dark hair, dark eyes, flawless bone structure, perfectly symmetrical features and a body worthy of any romance book cover, Leviathan had a too-perfect, granite statue kind of beauty that made him both hard to look at and hard to look away from. He wore a flowy white shirt, metal plated leather pants and a wide smile that showed his long, glistening white fangs. I might've drooled over him if he didn't scare the ever-loving shit out of me.

"Hello, Leviathan," I said.

"I thought I told you to call me Levi."

I scrunched up my face. We were not friends.

"Please."

I didn't want to. If I started calling him cute nicknames, I ran the risk of forgetting just how powerful and dangerous he could be. No one knew exactly what kind of glamy Leviathan was or where he came from. Some sites on the internet hypothesized he was part beast and controlled the barghests who roamed the veil. Others claimed he was the first original necromancer and became lost in the veil because he didn't have an anchor to bring him back. He survived by using the souls of the dead and other lost necromancers to sustain him and over time he transformed into something else.

Some raunchy fanfiction claimed he was a naughty fae capable of devious bedroom acts, and other sources claimed he was a god, banished for past transgressions, forever held apart from his brethren.

At the end of the day, who or what Leviathan was or wasn't didn't matter. Not if I was dead. There was no point in pursuing that information either. At least not yet. Especially not right now. I needed to focus on getting away first.

"Did you seriously send a spirit after me?" I asked.

Leviathan cocked his head. "How could you even think that? If I recall correctly, you're the one who called him."

But Johnny had been prepped. Leviathan had given the cheating bastard orders before I called him to the living realm. That meant Leviathan either held some sort of control over all the souls in the veil or he detected my call in advance and somehow reached Johnny before I drew him to the living realm.

How did he know I'd summon Johnny tonight? Or at all? Was he capable of spying on the living realm? Could he travel there? Or...

Sometimes the simplest answer was the most probable answer.

"Did you command *all* the spirits to haul me to the

veil with them if I called them to the living realm?" I asked.

"I was motivated to see you again." Leviathan shrugged as if it were no big deal. Maybe it wasn't to him, but to me, it showed immense power that eclipsed my own. "You owe me a favour, after all."

"Okay, I'm here." I stepped back from Leviathan to give us more space. He was too close, and I was already mentally freaking out.

If Leviathan commanded the souls so easily, he could haul me to the veil anytime he wanted. Anytime. Death raisers raised the dead. I couldn't and wouldn't stop. It was like telling a caffeine addict to stop drinking coffee because one day, one cup might taste bad.

Okay...that was me, too. I was the caffeine addict.

"What would you like to discuss?" I asked.

"Our date, of course."

My brain misfired. "I'm sorry, what?"

"I'd like to talk about our date."

"We don't have one."

"We will soon. What would you like to do?"

I dropped my hands to my side and settled on blinking at the Lord of the Veil. Mom used to say when it rained, it poured, but this was unheard of. At least for me. First, Kang asked me out, finally, and now this guy?

"Why on Earth would you want to date me?" I blurted out.

"We're not on Earth," he pointed out.

This felt like all kinds of wrong. Leviathan might be attractive in the same way a dragon would be beautiful even as it burned my entire world down around me, but we'd only had a brief interaction in the past. I knew nothing about him aside from the cautionary bedtime stories and those were not exactly great recommendations. And then there was that pesky problem regarding his true motivations.

He didn't want to date me for me. He couldn't. He hadn't had a chance to know me. And though I didn't want to sell myself short in the looks department, I'd never been the striking, I'm-going-to-fall-for-you-at-first-sight kind of hot. If he wanted some arm candy, surely there were easier, more willing options.

Which meant my skills as a necromancer had something to do with his interest. I wasn't a jackass, no matter what my brother said when he was angry. This guy wanted me at least partly, if not solely, because of my magic.

"I'm going to respectfully decline. Thank you," I said and held my breath. During the last case, I'd brought the evil killing spirit to the veil and made a deal with Leviathan. He'd take care of the spirit and ensure it never travelled back to the living realm, and I'd owe him a favour. I hadn't planned to return to the veil so soon, if at all, but now that I was here, now that he'd made a point of showing me he could bring me here pretty much whenever he wanted, I had to face the awful truth that he might call in the favour at any time and I'd be helpless to prevent it.

He cocked his head. Death magic swirled around us. "You're saying no?"

"Well, you didn't exactly phrase it as a question in the first place, which is part of the problem. Women usually like to be asked, not ordered."

"From my experience, women like being told things," he grumbled.

"Like what?" I placed my hands on my hips. Leviathan must be more isolated from reality than I originally thought, despite having access to a constant stream of incoming souls.

"They like being told they're a *good girl*." His lips quirked.

Okay, maybe he wasn't isolated at all, but I wasn't going to comment on that, even if my body shivered at the rumble of his words.

Last time I checked, I didn't have a praise kink, but he made it sound like something I definitely wanted to hear again.

I just wanted someone else to say it.

"Have you visited the living realm in the last decade or two?" I asked, instead. Hoping he didn't catch my physical reaction.

His gaze flashed and he leaned forward. The souls wailed around him and sped away in the wind. "I cannot walk through the portals I create. I can only visit when called and it has been a long time since my feet felt the hot soil under the sun."

Guess that answered one of my questions.

No necromancers that I knew of ever came across Leviathan in the veil. Hell, most of them couldn't travel to the veil in the first place. When I met Leviathan and he formed a portal for me to return to the living realm, I thought maybe he also used the portals for himself to sneak off and live his best life amongst the drabs.

He'd just shot down that theory.

Not only was he not hiding amid the drabs and glamies, but he also couldn't travel to the living realm at all unless called.

"Is that why you're asking me out?" I asked. "Hoping for a one-way ticket to the humans."

He narrowed his eyes. "I asked you out because you're the first female necromancer I've encountered who can travel to the veil unhindered, with ease, and keep your sanity. This might come as a surprise to you, but this place gets lonely, and I'd like to get to know you better. The spirits tell me the way to do that is to ask you out on a date."

Oh.

That actually sounded reasonable.

It also sounded like I was being asked out because I was the only option, but at least I understood his motivations better.

Kang's disgruntled face popped into my mind and guilt twisted my stomach. We weren't dating. We hadn't even gone out. But I already knew how he'd feel if I dated someone else at the same time, even if we weren't technically exclusive.

"So?" Leviathan asked.

"I'll think about it," I said.

Total lie. I didn't want to date Leviathan. I wanted Kang's grumpy ass.

But I couldn't say no to Leviathan again. Not right now. Not here. Not when I was in his domain and at his mercy. My bond with the master vampire was weakening and without it, I couldn't pull myself free of the veil. So I told Leviathan I'd think about it and in a way I would. I'd think about all the reasons why I wouldn't say yes.

"And that's all I ask," Leviathan said. He waved his hand and a portal to the graveyard opened. "As a sign of good faith."

T he light streaming in the room teased my face and pulled me from a delectable dream featuring one grumpy detective, myself and a night of no inhibitions where I was told I was a *very* good girl.

Heat flushed my face, and I turned over in the bed to check the time on my phone.

A single, plump red rose sat on the nightstand beside my charging base. Cold struck my body like a lightning bolt. I jerked upright, the bedding falling off me, and scanned my room.

Nothing.

I was alone.

Brandon and Logan talked in hushed voices in the living room and the regular backdrop of traffic drifted in from the street outside our building. The soft scents of vanilla and rose petals clung to the air.

I reached forward and plucked the rose off the nightstand. It had a long stem and stunning petals almost bursting with colour. It was just as beautiful as the rose left outside the apartment door.

And yet, this rose wasn't scary.

It was terrifying.

Someone had snuck into our apartment and my room, undetected, to place this on my bedside table without waking me or the boys.

Maggie meowed outside my door, letting me know in a particularly high-pitched shrieking sound that I needed to feed her.

My gaze snagged on my bedroom door.

The simple answer lay on the other side of this wall. Not my cat...my roommates.

I flung the bedding off my legs, hopped from the bed, threw my door open and stomped into the living room. Maggie hissed and raced off to hide, her desperate all-consuming need for food momentarily forgotten.

Logan and Brandon stopped their conversation, their mouths comically hanging open as they turned toward me.

"What the fuck, guys?" I waved the rose in the air. "Leaving one outside our apartment may have been ha-ha funny to you, but this has gone far enough. I just lost ten years off my life from a fucking flower."

Brandon frowned and pushed his curly brown hair from his face. Tall, rugged, and built like a linebacker, my brother's boyfriend had raised the bar considerably for my expectations of a partner. "What are you talking about?"

Logan vibrated. His normally blue eyes darkened to almost black and a chill spread over the room. He was a taller, stronger, male version of myself, including the black-brown hair, fair skin, and attitude problem. He hadn't inherited the family's necromancer magic. He'd received something else entirely, something darker that he rarely spoke about. Whatever his skillset, he wasn't a drab and he excelled at killing people for a living.

Brandon side-eyed his boyfriend and stepped away.

"Where did you find that?" Logan asked, his voice a low rumble full of malice.

"Bedside table." I kept waving the rose between us, but my confidence quickly faded. "Where you left it."

"We didn't leave the flower, Sparky." Logan took two steps to close the distance between us and snatched the rose from my hand. He studied the petals and the stem and then sniffed it. He narrowed his eyes and stalked past me to my bedroom leaving me to trade panicked looks with Brandon.

"You two aren't fucking with me?" I whispered the question.

Brandon shook his head, concern etched into his brow.

I followed Logan, padding back to my room.

Folding my arms over my chest, I leaned on the door frame and watched my twin stomp around. He flung open the closet door. Not finding anything, he stomped to the other side of my room, viciously pulled up the blinds and threw the window open. I cringed with each sound, half-expecting something to snap.

"Do you think the point of entry was my window?" I asked. "I'm sure I would've heard that or felt the draft."

Logan scowled over his shoulder and peered out the window. With a curse, he spun around. His gaze dropped to my desk. He sputtered. The fury raging behind his eyes momentarily disappeared. "What's this?"

"Dad's case file." I looked at it last night after returning from the veil. The original detectives had done little leg work, but the added documentation indicated Kang had been very thorough in chasing down every single lead mentioned in the original report. He'd interviewed work colleagues and friends, and he did so without any of us knowing. Nothing in the report screamed "smoking gun" to solve Dad's disappearance, but my heart did funny things as I read through the reports. Kang cared a lot.

"Your cop boyfriend give you this?" Logan leafed through the top few sheets.

"He's not my boyfriend, but yes."

"You need to let it go, Sparky." His gaze met mine, momentarily clear and blue. "You need to let him go."

"Kang?"

"No." Logan's scowl deepened. "Dad."

I shook my head, my messy hair smacking my face. "You need to let me deal with Dad's disappearance my own way. I don't lecture you, so don't you dare try to scold me."

He grumbled, his attention already drifting away from the desk. He scanned the rest of my room and found nothing, because there was nothing to find, and shouldered his way past me to investigate the rest of the apartment.

"If you're not careful, he's going to lock you in a room until he's found and neutralized the threat," Brandon whispered.

I turned to find him right behind me, the concern still tugging his brows down.

"If you make a distraction, I'll slip out." I jerked my head toward Logan whose cursing grew louder and louder. He had searched his own room, the main bathroom, the entryway closet, and now examined our main entrance door and its locks.

"Did you put the chain on last night?" he growled over his shoulder.

"No, did you?" I called back.

He swore.

"I didn't either, so you can add me to the shit list," Brandon offered.

I reached out and rubbed his arm. "No one's adding you to a shit list."

We exchanged small smiles.

I left Logan to rage-search our apartment and Brandon to supervise while I slipped back into my room to get dressed and run a brush through my tangled hair. My supervisor and work friend Denise had already sent me a text to remind me about the home-visit appointment I had in an hour.

I threw on my classic necromancer all-leather outfit and stepped out of the bedroom. I left my purse on the kitchen counter and fed Maggie. She was still hiding, but food always perked her up. The kibble hit the tiny metal dish and a cooing meow trickled into the kitchen moments before Maggie padded into the room. She bumped into my leg, arching her back and rubbing her furry body into my calf, before heading to the food bowl. I leaned down and scratched her behind the ears.

"Sorry for scaring you," I said.

A loud purr erupted from her fluffy white body before she started munching on her food.

A whisper of death magic flittered across the room and when I straightened, I came face to face with a ghost.

Bernie was Maggie's former owner—or servant, depending on who you asked. She popped in from time to time, still fueled with the love she had for her cat. Sometimes, she even spoke to me, though those moments were less and less as her power dwindled. She'd travel to the veil soon, and I'd miss her.

Not only had Bernie tipped me off about my last

boyfriend's nasty habit of sticking his dick in other women, she'd also been a constant, positive presence in my life. The last time she'd spoken, though, she gave me a warning. "He's seen you," she'd said, though she couldn't tell me his name.

"Hey, Bernie," I said. "Good to see you again."

She nodded and drifted down to her cat.

Maggie stopped eating and looked up at the ghost and purred louder.

"Do you know the name of the man I should be careful around?" I asked. "The man you warned me about?"

Bernie looked up from petting Maggie and shook her head.

"Do you know who left me roses?"

She shook her head again.

Dammit. Worth a shot.

Maggie rubbed her face into Bernie's and her purr intensified. Bernie looked up at me again, a tear falling from her eye.

"Can't speak?"

She shook her head.

"Was it harder coming back this time?"

She nodded and more tears spilled down her face.

Pain struck my chest. "I'll take care of her, Bernie. I promise. She'll know only love until she's ready to meet you again."

Bernie bobbed her head, tears flowing down her face, her body shaking. She faded away.

Maggie meowed at the empty air, calling for her friend.

I straightened and wiped the tears that had escaped my own eyes. Great. I had to go to work and now all I wanted to do was cry. I snatched my purse from the kitchen counter and headed toward the door.

"Where the fuck do you think you're going?" Logan growled from the living room.

"I have to work."

"There's someone sneaking into our apartment. It's not safe for you to go out."

"And it's safe for me to stay in?"

Logan snapped his mouth shut and glowered. "I'll fucking make it safe."

Brandon groaned.

"Logan..." I started.

He held his hand up to silence me.

"I will make it safe. No one will harm you. No one will scare you. I will kill anyone who tries."

I walked over to him and placed a hand on his shoulder. He vibrated with anger. "Thank you, but I'm still going out. I'm not helpless and I have a job to do."

He flashed his teeth like a wild animal warning off other animals. "You better take your boot knife."

"I have my boot knife, my ceremonial knife, my super-duper secret pant-sheathed knife, and my purse knife. I've got all my knives."

He jerked his chin up and down, appearing somewhat placated.

I spun away and walked quickly toward the door before he found more steam to renew the argument. Slinging my purse over my shoulder and grabbing my phone off the small table, I shouted a goodbye to the boys and headed out the door. Thankfully, no roses lay in the hallway.

My phone flashed, reminding me I had an unchecked voicemail. Peter had called me twice while I'd been in the veil, and I didn't need to hear the new voicemail to know he was worried about me. I'd straight up disappeared.

When I returned from the veil, Peter and the client had already left. I saw the missed calls and sent a quick text to let Peter know I was okay, but also knew that short response wouldn't be enough to appease his questions and need for an explanation. He was a lawyer after all.

Too bad I didn't have any answers—or at least none that I was willing to provide.

Instead, I attempted to keep my mind off all things Leviathan-related by staying busy.

I STOOD outside the apartment building on the corner of a busy intersection. In a typical city neighbourhood, the street bustled with traffic and a number of pedestrians walked along the sidewalk. The smell of vendor food filled the air.

I rang the buzzer for the client's apartment and waited. The sun heated my back and birds chirped in the nearby ornamental trees that lined the sidewalk. It was a beautiful day, but I was in a foul mood. After waking up to that rose, I really didn't have the patience to deal with a house call today.

"H...Hello?" A woman's nervous voice crackled through the speaker.

I leaned forward to speak into the intercom. "Hello, my name is Lark Morgan. I'm from Raisers."

"Come in. Turn right down the first hallway. I'm on the main floor."

The door buzzed and I reached forward to pull it open before it relocked. The glass door swung open with ease, and I walked through the lobby with shiny floor tiles and followed the woman's directions.

I normally met clients in cemeteries or in the office, but this client insisted on a home visit. These weren't unheard of, but I preferred to avoid them. If Denise hadn't bribed me with a chocolate bar and travel pay, I would be comfortably sitting in my office right now.

Still, home visits represented unknown factors and an elevated risk. I reached into my pocket to hold onto the can of bear spray. Sure, I had a number of knives strapped to my body, but wielding a sharp weapon always carried a risk. I might unnecessarily injure the other person or myself in an altercation.

That was why I often brought bear spray to home visits.

Mace might be illegal in Canada but thank goodness for hunters.

I stood outside the door and knocked. It swung open right away to reveal a petite woman with brown hair and eyes. She wore a loose white T-shirt and shorts. Not long board shorts, or shorts so short I'd have to look away if she turned around. Just regular, well-fitting shorts. "I'm Cathy."

"Hi, Cathy." I stood awkwardly at the apartment's entrance and released the bear spray in my pocket. My work clothes always came with that awful feeling of being overdressed.

"Please come in." Cathy waved her arm at the interior of her apartment.

I stepped into the apartment and let my magic flow down the hallway ahead of me. The power bounced off the walls, echoing back with disinterest. "There's no death in this home."

"Not yet." Cathy shivered as she stepped past me and led the way to the living room. Two large windows looked out to the street corners outside. Because the windows were on two adjoining walls, Cathy had a view of both streets and where they met at the intersection.

Solid iron bars lined the windows for security but somehow looked stylish instead of coming across like we were in a jail cell. A magnetic gray couch sat under one of the windows while a matching armchair was positioned under the other. A small table had been placed in the corner, and a book rested open on its smooth wooden surface, spine up.

"Would you like something to drink? Coffee, perhaps?" Cathy twisted her fingers together.

"No, thank you." I waved at the giant windows. "Nice view."

Cathy turned to consider the windows. "That's why you're here."

I frowned. "The report said very little aside from this being a ghost consult."

Cathy shrugged but continued to study the view. "It's hard to explain without everyone thinking I'm ridiculous."

"Well, now's your opportunity to try."

Cathy nodded. "She appears once a month. At first, I thought I imagined things. Then I thought it might be a trick of the light or something to do with the moon cycle. But as far as I can tell, it's always on or near the twentieth of each month."

"That *she* appears."

"Yes."

"Who is she?"

"I don't know." Cathy finally turned away from the windows, her body shaking with nerves. "But I know what she is."

I raised an eyebrow and waited.

"She's a ghost and she's haunting the street corner."

I let Cathy's words sink in. Normally, spirits weren't visible to drabs but in some instances, if their death was traumatic enough or they had a lot of power prior to death, they had the ability to make themselves visible to anyone. If their deaths were horrific, the power of their demise fueled them to become ghosts— spirits stuck in the living realm like Bernie.

"There's a ghost that appears once or twice a month on your street corner?" I asked.

"Yes."

"Is it harassing you?"

"No."

"Is it malicious in any way?"

"I don't know for sure, but I think so." Cathy sighed and sat down on the gray couch. She waved at the opposite armchair, but I shook my head. I preferred to stand. "I started to dig a little. This intersection has a disproportionately high incidence of accidents."

"What kind of accidents?" I peered out the window again.

"All kinds. Collisions, pedestrians getting hit. Cyclists getting clipped."

"Okay..."

"You think I'm ridiculous."

I shook my head. "Not at all. I'm just wondering why you called in a necromancer. There isn't a body to raise. I'm not sure how you expect me to help. This seems like more of a job for a generalized witch. The local coven might have someone they can refer."

Though necromancers were derogatively referred to as bone witches, we got our own glamy subcategory due to where we drew our power from and our connection with the spirit realm. Generalized witches used spells and herbs and though they had magic in their blood, they weren't connected to the veil. Their power was derived solely from the living realm.

Cathy nodded at my suggestion before responding. "There isn't a body to raise, you're right. But you don't need to raise her. She's already here. You can speak to her, right? I read that necromancers can see and speak to spirits."

Technically, anyone could speak to a spirit, they just couldn't see the spirits or hear their responses without the aid of a necromancer and that made conversation a little one-sided and difficult to navigate. But as a necromancer, I saw spirits regardless of whether they chose to be visible, and they also tended to be drawn to me. The death magic flowing in my veins made most spirits want to do whatever I asked.

Most.

A rampaging, murderous spirit from the last police case I consulted on had no qualms with ignoring me completely.

"That's correct," I answered, not bothering to get into the technicalities. "But without the bones, I can't control her."

"I don't want you to control her. I just want you to talk to her and find out what she wants. Maybe she'll move on without you having to assist her," Cathy said. "Or maybe if we can find out who she is, we can locate her bones and help her to the veil that way."

I sighed. Speaking to a spirit without control could be dangerous depending on the spirit, but it was worth finding out a bit more.

"I'll look into it."

"The twentieth is coming up. She usually appears around two in the morning."

I nodded and mentally went through what I needed to do to prepare for meeting a potentially dangerous spirit. "I'll be here."

CHAPTER
SIX

I stood outside my apartment building and fished in my purse for my keys. Apparently, a lot of women got attacked and abducted outside their buildings and vehicles, and it wasn't hard to see why with my arm elbow deep in the abyss of my bag while leaning down to get a closer look.

Perfect time to attack.

Instead, my phone rang. I gave up on my keys and grabbed the phone. The call display said, "Mom" with three hearts on each side.

I hit accept and held the phone to my ear. "Hi, Mom."

"Darling! How are you?" Mom's normally thin, craggy voice held energy and excitement.

"I think the more important thing to ask is, how are you?" I sat down on the bench outside the apartment's entrance. "You sound amazing."

"I feel amazing," she said.

"Did Gregor come to see you tonight?" The Master Vampire of Victoria had agreed to clean Mom's blood with his own. This treatment was more effective than any of the costly medical ones I'd been saving for with my brother. Not many vampires willingly gave blood, but Gregor did because he got me in exchange.

For every healing session, I raised a baby vampire.

I wasn't an expert in vampires by any means, but when one was freshly made, they went in the ground to sleep for an indeterminate amount of time. Some took a few days, some months, and some, often the more powerful ones, took years.

And then some never woke from their vampiric slumber. These freshly made vampires were essentially another vampire's offspring and losing their children to the soil was upsetting to say the least.

I had the ability to find the soul of the slumbering vampires in the veil and help them rise.

The act was not without risk.

I had to use my own blood instead of a sacrifice and had to travel to the veil where baghests ran around, and Leviathan not only ruled but waited with dating propositions.

Each time I travelled to the veil, I risked not returning.

"I did see Gregor," Mom answered. "His blood is liquid magic."

I cringed but didn't disagree. Gregor's blood wasn't

a cure, but it would buy the scientific community more time to find one, or at least give Mom an extended lease on life. It had already significantly improved her quality of life and I would do it all over again to hear the energy and excitement in her voice.

Gregor's blood also protected me in the veil and safeguarded me from becoming lost. The anchoring didn't last forever, though, only the lifespan of the blood, and as I'd discovered in the veil already, the bond had weakened significantly.

"That's awesome, Mom." I'd raised two baby vamps for Gregor and Mom had just received her second treatment. If she needed more or if I wanted to renew my bond with Gregor, I'd have to visit the vampires again.

I shuddered. I didn't dislike the vampires. They had treated me well. But I'd recently learned my necromancer skills were strong enough to control them and that little fact was just enough to outweigh my usefulness to them and get me killed.

"And how is Gregor tonight?" I asked, placing my purse on my lap to start digging for my keys again.

"Oh, he's such a gentleman. I can't thank you enough. Three treatments and I feel like I'm twenty again."

I froze, my hand on my wallet. "Did you say three?"

Mom paused. "Yes..."

I bit back a curse. My phone buzzed with a text message, and I pulled it away from my ear to read it.

You owe me a payment, Gregor wrote.

"Motherfucker."

"Is everything okay?" Mom asked.

"Yes, of course." I scrambled with how to say the next part. I didn't want Mom to feel like she'd done something wrong, or that I didn't want to make the payments. But I also didn't want Gregor to use Mom to get me into his debt irrevocably. "Gregor and I have a pay-per-play kind of deal. I already agreed to the third payment, so this isn't a big deal." A small lie wouldn't hurt anyone. "But I worry he might try to take advantage of our lack of communication."

"You're worried he'll place you in his debt?" Mom asked.

"Exactly. I will gladly pay the fees, all the fees, for your treatment, Mom. They're within me to pay, but let's be careful and not let Gregor pull some sneaky vampire shit."

"You got it," Mom said. "I love you."

"Love you, too." I said goodbye and hung up the call. Without hesitating, I dialled Gregor right away.

"Ms. Morgan, what a pleasure to hear from you this evening. How can I help you?"

"I'm glad you asked. In the future, I would appreciate it if you would wait to provide my mom with treatment until after I've paid for said treatment."

"Ah, Ms. Morgan, I can hear the concern in your

voice. I regret to inform you that this was not a part of our original agreement. We said one raising per treatment. There was nothing in the phrasing about restricting or specifying the order of the payment and treatment. Nor did any wording prevent the possibility of providing new treatment before the previous one was paid."

I scowled at my phone. I'd raise as many vampires as I had to for Mom's continued health. But if I wasn't careful, Gregor could perform additional, unnecessary treatments that I would end up spending the rest of my life trying to pay for. And what if he stalled, not letting me raise any of his vampires right away? What happened then? He could arguably turn me into a human servant just to ensure I kept my end of the deal. I needed tight control on this agreement so I didn't end up indentured.

"Our agreement also allowed for renegotiation," I said carefully. "May I humbly ask that you treat my mother only after I've raised a vampire for you?"

"You may ask." He paused dramatically.

I cursed silently, I'd already asked nicely, said please and everything. I'd beg if I had to, but I knew enough about Gregor to know it wouldn't matter.

"If I ask again and say pretty please with a cherry on top, will you please withhold treatment until after I pay?" I asked anyway, fully knowing the answer.

Gregor chuckled. "Absolutely not. Our agreement

might allow renegotiation, but I'm under no obligation to accept any new terms."

I sighed. At least the master vampire was predictable. "Separate topic. Have you been leaving me roses?"

Gregor laughed. "Should I have?"

"Absolutely not."

"Maybe you have a secret admirer."

Yeah, I'd rather not have one that snuck into my room at night while I slept, but I didn't share that detail with Gregor. If I reached out to anyone, it would be Kang. My brother already knew, and he was probably still fortifying our apartment and making plans to imprison me in my room while he slaughtered anyone who came close to our home.

Fuck. I'd have to tell Kang. I'd promised, after all.

"Have you travelled to the veil lately?" Gregor asked, bumping me from my thoughts. "I thought I felt a tug."

Subtle. Gregor casually reminded me I needed him as an anchor—just in case I had any thoughts of calling off our deal entirely. "Yeah. That was unexpected."

"Yet, you've returned and you didn't require help. At least not from me."

"Leviathan turned up." The Lord of the Veil was the reason I got pulled from the living realm in the first place, but I preferred to keep that little morsel of information to myself. It seemed like something Gregor would try to use against me.

"And he didn't kill you instantly and drain your blood?" Gregor sounded more amused than surprised.

"He's not a vampire, Gregor." At least, I didn't think he was.

Come to think of it, he did have fangs.

Crap.

"Wait," I said. Maybe Gregor had some information I wasn't privy to. "Is he?"

Gregor hummed and didn't answer right away.

"Gregor?"

He sighed. "We don't know. It's one of the many possible explanations for his origin and existence. Maybe he is. Maybe he isn't. Or maybe he's a little of everything."

"He has fangs."

"A lot of things have fangs, Ms. Morgan," Gregor said. "Did he have the book?"

Now it was my turn to sigh. Prickling unease crept along my spine. It seemed like a lifetime ago I'd unwittingly helped take the infamous Book of the Dead to the veil. Gregor had helped me return to the living realm, and once he learned what had been in my possession, he'd become interested. Very interested.

The Book of the Dead had been known as the Book of Life at one time and was rumoured to hold the key to freeing vampires from their nightly constraints.

"He didn't have the book on him," I said.

"Do you know where he keeps it?"

"Of course not! Nor do I intend to find out." I

spotted my house keys in the abyss of my purse and snatched them before the vortex sucked them back up again.

"You've made your position on the matter clear," Gregor said. "Please forgive me for attempting to gather information on a matter of great importance and personal significance."

"Oh, stop it," Estelle hissed somewhere in the background on Gregor's side of the line. "Hand the phone over."

"*Chouchou*," Gregor pleaded, but he must've relented because the next person to speak into the phone was Estelle.

Estelle Beaumont was Gregor's human servant. Gorgeous, and somehow, despite being surrounded by scary, powerful vampires who took themselves very seriously, she was nice. Friendly, even. I'd appreciated her empathy when Gregor had brought me to his home and I was unsure of my fate. We'd gone out for coffee a couple of times since then—not enough for me to consider her a friend, but enough for me to know I wanted her as one.

"Enough of this business talk," Estelle said. "I've been dying to get out of this viper den. Do you have plans for the rest of the evening?"

Well, I'd planned to sleep for the next decade, but I'd change my plans for a chance to hang out with Estelle. "What do you have in mind?"

The heavy bass made my heart feel like it tried to punch through my rib cage. A throng of people writhed on the dance floor, swaying, and gyrating to the beat and attempting to hump each other with their clothes on.

Spiral had an interesting layout. Booths lined the entirety of one wall and a long bar lined the opposite side. A large square shaped dance floor took up the bulk of the club. A DJ with spiky blue and green hair did her thing on a raised stage at the end of the room. Stairs to the left of the stage led to bathrooms downstairs and stairs to the right led to a second floor where Grant Malone, the owner of the club had his office, security room, and wrap around balcony that surrounded the entirety of the dance floor.

I'd danced with Kang on that floor. My body heated from the memory. Dancing with the grumpy detective had been powerful enough to tell me four things—we had chemistry, he could move exceptionally well, he wanted me, and I wanted him.

I'd probably wanted him for years, but that dance had smacked my face with the truth. What I'd mistaken for irritation and loathing was something deeper and scarier, something that made my chest tighten and my heart flutter.

All those years of angsty hatred hid the deeply repressed need to feel that man moving his body with mine.

"Why did you choose this place?" I yelled over the music. I needed to get my mind off Kang. No one wanted to hang out with a sucker daydreaming about someone else.

Estelle had gotten us into the popular club, bypassing the long line outside, and secured a private booth, but it was still hard to have a conversation. Two of Gregor's vampires stood guard, watching the club, and deterring anyone ignorant enough to try to approach the Master Vampire of Victoria's human servant and personal necromancer.

Not that anyone outside Gregor's inner circle knew I worked for him and hopefully, no one ever did —I'd lose my day job and contract work with the VicPD didn't cover rent on its own.

I didn't know one of the guards—a tall woman with a sharp gaze and a perpetually serious expression plastered on her face—but the other was Pierre Deveau, the first vampire I'd raised for Gregor. Despite Pierre wearing modern day clothes, like the expensive suit he had on right now, he still looked like he should be in a ballroom dancing with Marie Antoinette, not at a modern club with scantily clad drabs rubbing against each other.

He had brown hair that fell in soft waves past his shoulders and honey-coloured eyes that softened whenever his gaze met mine. Maybe I just had a soft spot for the first vampire I'd raised, but I felt connected to Pierre. Gregor had never revealed how long the newly risen vampire had been in the ground, his soul lost in the veil, nor did he elaborate why Pierre was so special to be chosen out of all the vampires on Gregor's estate.

Whatever the case, Pierre had greeted me with a wide smile and treated me like a queen alongside Estelle.

"Are you kidding me? Why wouldn't I pick this place?" Estelle yelled over her martini glass. With her tight curls pulled back into a chic twisty bun thing, and naturally striking face, she made this place classier with her presence, even with the leather miniskirt and matching bustier. "Spiral is the hottest club right now."

I shrugged. How would I know that? I only went where my brother and his boyfriend dragged me.

"The owner is rumoured to be a witch. Gregor has him under surveillance," Estelle added.

"Really? I didn't get witch vibes from Grant."

Estelle's eyebrows shot up. "You've met Victoria's most eligible bachelor?"

Eligible? I sipped my crantini to hide my scowl. "Danced with him, too."

Estelle reached out and smacked my arm. "Shut up. Really? How was it?"

"Oh, let's just say I doubt he'll ever forget me or the experience any time soon."

Estelle frowned, her perfect brows dipping down and rippling her flawless brown skin. "I feel like there's more to this story."

"There is."

"But you won't share?" She took a sip of her martini.

"Tit for tat, buttercup. I want to know about you. I'm fairly certain your stories are much more entertaining than mine about dancing with some random club owner."

Estelle's smile widened and her large brown eyes lit up. "I do have a few stories."

"Perfect. Pick one and we'll start there."

Estelle laughed. She had a nice laugh, not the boisterous loud kind that made me wince, nor the soft, almost fake tittering sound more akin to a bell that made me want to smack something. Estelle had a nice warm laugh that brought a smile to my face, and I very much wanted her to be my friend.

I didn't have a lot of friends. I had friends in school mostly because I hid what I could do with my magic.

When I grew up and came into my power, I quickly discovered the strength of those friendships—or lack thereof. No one ever talked about how hard it was to make friends as an adult. At least, that was the vibe in Victoria. From what I heard, Vancouver was even worse.

As I soon found out, most adults didn't want to make new friends when they already had a safe, core group from school, and they especially didn't want to hang out with someone who killed farm animals to raise dead people and slept through most of the day. I worked absurd hours and had magical abilities that made most people uncomfortable, drabs and glamies alike. My friends consisted of Denise from work, my brother, and Brandon, and I was fine with that because I didn't often come across someone I wanted to be friends with. Until now.

"Is it offensive to ask a human servant their age?" I asked.

"It is if you're a stranger, and before you ask, no, we're not strangers." She smiled again. "I was born in 1792."

I choked on my crantini. "You're over two hundred years old?" I knew drinking vampire blood extended a human servant's life, but I always figured Estelle was younger for some reason.

"Of course. I'm one of the younger humans serving under a master vampire."

"Why are you hanging out with me? I can be

immature, even for my own age, but I must come across as infantile to you."

Estelle shook her head. "The key to looking young is feeling young."

"Here I thought it was vampire blood…"

Estelle snorted and her lips twitched. "It is, but even baby-faced vamps can come across ancient. I didn't become a human servant because I wanted to feel old and superior. I wanted to be young forever. Youth is my drug and you, my dear, have a boat load of it. I like to surround myself with people from all walks of life, at all stages, but most especially those in their prime."

"Thank you."

"For what?"

I placed my hand on my chest and batted my eyes. "For saying I'm in my prime." Actually, the thought was kind of sad. If this was me at my best, what did I have to look forward to?

Sitting back in the leather seat that creaked, I drank some more and studied Estelle over the rim of the glass. "So it was the love for eternal youth that led you to sign up to become a vampire's human servant?"

Estelle's smile faded and something shuttered in her gaze—an emotion so quick and intense, I couldn't identify it. "Not quite. That was a bit of a fib and one I hope you'll forgive me for. My entrance into the world of vampires is one story I'm not ready to share."

Most vampire stories weren't material for romance

movies, at least not the ones over a hundred years old that I'd read about. Of course, I could be mistaken. Up until Gregor approached me with a job opportunity, I'd steered clear of the vampire community and had to rely on rumours and internet searches as sources of information.

"That's okay," I said. "Why don't we start with how you met Gregor?"

"Ah, well. That story is one and the same, but I appreciate your attempt to steer the conversation to happier memories. Let me tell you about the time Gregor asked me to befriend a Canadian politician for our benefit."

She scooted over to my side of the bench so she didn't have to yell and I sat back to listen. It came as no surprise to me that Estelle had easily infiltrated the politician's inner circle and became the focus of his obsession. Her influence had been crucial to the law that recognized vampires as Canadian citizens.

What surprised me was the politician, quite elderly now, still sent her flowers even after it became apparent she had used him and that Estelle spoke with a kind fondness for the man. It hadn't all been an act.

"Relationships between humans and vampires aren't meant to last," Estelle explained. "The same can be said about a human servant and a human. Even if one sought to unnaturally prolong the relationship, the dynamics are never the same. It's easier to say goodbye than let a love linger and fester."

Ouch. That sounded rough.

"So, you were instrumental in developing the Vampire Act?" I frowned at my empty drink. When did I finish it?

"It was a group effort," she said, placing her empty glass beside mine. "Pierre, we need another round."

Pierre grinned in response and slipped into the crowd, the throng of humans parting for him. Apparently, Gregor never allowed bar staff to serve Estelle drinks when they were out. Too many things could happen to the beverage from the bar to the table, so the guards always acted as go-betweens. They watched the drinks get poured and then brought them straight to the table.

"That should've been my round," I said.

"Pffft. Let me get the drinks tonight." Estelle waved her hand in the air royally.

"Ladies." A familiar voice spoke at the edge of the table where Pierre had stood. The other guard had shifted to the side to watch the club owner as the newcomer spoke to us.

Grant wore a gray suit and a crisp white collared shirt with just enough buttons undone to show off his gold chain and toned, tanned chest. He'd slicked his dark hair back with gel.

"I hope you're enjoying your night." His gaze flicked between us.

Surprisingly, he didn't flinch when he met my gaze. "Always a pleasure to see you, Ms. Morgan."

Pierre returned and slid our drinks across the table. He frowned at the owner, but Estelle nodded, and he moved to the side to resume his post. The other guard followed suit. They might have their backs turned to the table, but they could hear every word spoken and one wrong move from Grant and he'd find himself in some deep trouble that being a club owner wouldn't get him out of.

"Does your partner know you're here?" Grant asked me.

I took a sip of my new crantini and used the moment to collect my thoughts before answering. "I'm not a cop, Mr. Malone, and even if I was, I don't need permission to have a life."

"I wasn't referring to that kind of partner, Ms. Morgan."

Oh.

"I saw the security footage of the two of you." He shrugged as if the images of me dancing with Kang and basically having sex with clothes on didn't bother him, but the tension in his hands gave him away.

"Imagine my surprise," he said. "Your dancing skills magically improved."

"Did you not enjoy our dance together?" I batted my eyelashes. Look at me. Super bold with two vampires and a human servant to back me up.

Instead of scowling, Grant smiled slowly. "Let's just say, watching you with him gave me something to aspire to."

Estelle watched the entire exchange with an impassive expression and sipped her martini.

Grant turned to her and performed a weird half-bow. "Please pass along my well-wishes to Gregor. Your table will be taken care of tonight by me personally." He stepped back and opened his arms out. "Please enjoy the rest of your evening."

Estelle waited until Grant disappeared in the jumble of dancers before snorting. "I take it you didn't perform satisfactorily when you danced with him?"

Estelle was quick.

"That's putting it mildly."

"And then, to rub salt into the wound, you danced with a cop and showed Grant what you could really do?"

"That wasn't my intention, but yeah. He would've seen the footage and figured out I had purposefully stomped on him."

Estelle lifted her glass and smiled. "I knew I liked you."

I clinked Estelle's glass with my own before taking a sip.

"Now. Tell me about this cop." Estelle leaned back in the booth. "It's your turn to share a story, after all. Tit for tat, buttercup."

I choked on my drink. Kang was the last thing I wanted to talk about...even if he was constantly on my mind.

EIGHT

With Pierre holding the door open, I stepped into the calm ambience of the dimly lit café that sat across the street from Spiral. The warm air surrounded me, and I paused to deeply inhale the scents of rich, freshly brewed coffee and baked goods. When I opened my eyes, I found Pierre looking at me oddly.

"Are you okay?" he asked.

"I love coffee," I said.

He pursed his lips and glanced at the menu. "Things have changed an awful lot since I went in the ground."

I frowned. Pierre might be French, but he went into the ground in Victoria, BC, not France, so he unlikely predated the introduction of coffee to Western Europe. I had a hard time imagining Gregor and his posse being a part of the fur trade. But Pierre definitely predated cafés on every corner and cell phones in everyone's hands. He certainly held the phone Gregor had gifted him oddly and still texted with as many fingers as possible.

A barista stepped up to the counter and reached over with a white cloth to wipe the surface. He had a familiar face. "What can I get you guys?"

Where did I know this guy from?

The memory clicked in place.

Right. The same barista had served me and Kang when we were busy chasing that angry, murdering spirit. We ended up catching the spirit, but the necromancer who raised him was still a mystery.

What was the barista's name again? He'd made a point of telling me when we were here, and Kang had accused me of breaking hearts wherever I went.

The barista waited. He had a lean, wiry build and stood around six feet tall. Brown hair curled around his ears, and he wore a black collared shirt with the top two buttons unfastened to show off a chest tattoo and gold chain. He was pleasant enough to look at, but right now, the only one stirring any kind of heat in my blood was a grumpy detective.

God, I was pathetic.

"It's a latté, right?" the barista asked.

I rocked back on my heels. I mean, he was right...

"I never forget a pretty face." He flashed me a wide smile.

Estelle elbowed me in the side and lifted her

eyebrows. Yeah, I wasn't picking up a barista tonight, even if it meant he probably loved coffee as much as I did.

"You have a great memory. I'd love a latté, thank you," I said. "And before my friends try to pay, this is on me."

Estelle tsked and Pierre frowned. The other guard —name still unknown—just grunted. She probably wasn't going to drink any coffee anyway.

"Of course," the barista said before turning to Estelle. "And what can I get you?"

"I'll have the same, please." Estelle glanced at the two vampires who promptly shook their heads. "And that will be all."

The barista nodded and told me the total. I paid by slapping my credit card against a machine a couple of times before it dinged to let me know it had successfully taken my money.

"I'll bring the drinks out to you," the barista said.

"Thanks." I turned to discover Estelle and the female vampire guard had gone ahead to find seats while Pierre had stayed behind with me.

"You go ahead, *ma belle*," Pierre said. "I'll bring the drinks out."

Right. Estelle was only served by Gregor's guards.

The barista did a double take, but I wasn't about to apologize for the Master Vampire of Victoria taking necessary precautions to protect his human servant. I shrugged and offered him a small smile before leaving to join Estelle and Guard Number Two.

The warm lights hanging from the ceiling by chains cast a cozy glow over the room, and despite the late hour, over half the tables were occupied. The sounds of low chatter, clinking cups and the gurgle and hiss of the espresso machine filled the air.

Instead of sitting at one of the pedestal tables by the windows where I'd sat with Kang, Estelle had chosen one of the booths along the back wall. The other guard had taken her place, standing with her back to the table to watch the café.

I stopped short and peered up at her—a tall woman with a strong build and sharp features. "What's your name?"

I had asked earlier, but she refused to answer, pretending not to hear me over the loud music. She had no such excuse now and I wanted to know.

She jerked back and peered down at me.

"Because right now, I'm mentally referring to you as Guard Number Two, and that's just not right."

"Little death raiser, my name is Antonia."

I sputtered. Little death raiser. I was above average in height, thank you very much.

Estelle giggled and waved at me to join her in the booth. "Antonia isn't a talker. I'm surprised you got that much out of her."

True enough, the vampire guard had returned her

gaze to scanning the café for danger, the little death raiser forgotten.

I scooted over in the red leather seat with ornate brass fixtures and shared a smile with Estelle.

"So...*little death raiser*..." Laughter continued to dance in Estelle's gaze. "We no longer have to yell over the music. It's time to dish all your secrets."

I snorted and leaned back against the padded seat. Heat still danced in my veins from the drinks and my muscles twitched from all the dancing. "What secrets?"

Estelle pressed her lips together and hummed. "Well, you won't talk about the detective." She paused and waggled her eyebrows. When I remained silent, she sighed dramatically before continuing. "What else is going on in your life?"

"Someone has been leaving me roses."

She perked up at that.

"But it's not the hot cop and it's not my brother messing with me. And the last one was left inside my apartment." I shivered. "My brother is already livid and installing security cameras and I'm pretty sure he's doing sweeps of the area and will probably attempt to lock me in a padded room at some point. I'll have to tell Kang, too, and that won't go down well. I'm not looking forward to the conversation, but I'm not going to stay silent and let some stalker kill me, either."

"Kang?" She smiled widely, without showing teeth and for a second, she reminded me of a cat just settling down in a patch of sunlight—like she'd start purring any moment. "Is Connor Kang *your* detective?"

"You're insufferable."

"And I already know which detective is yours, Lark. Gregor thoroughly investigates those he considers his." She winked as if that shouldn't freak me out.

"Does he know who's sending me roses?" He'd told me he hadn't sent any flowers and I had no reason to believe he lied, though we spoke over the phone, not in person. Had it been in person, I would've had a better feel for the truth. My magic wasn't technically a lie detector, but I always sensed when the dead tried to lie to me. The magic flared and felt stickier in the air. I had no idea if I could detect a lie from a vampire, but vampires were dead, after all, and whenever I spoke to Gregor, the death magic surrounding him remained constant.

But just because he didn't lie, didn't mean he couldn't mislead. If he had me followed or investigated, he might very well know things I didn't—like my rose-stalker's identity.

Estelle opened her mouth to answer my question, but, just then, Pierre arrived with our drinks. Antonia moved to the side to give him room to slide the two lattes across the table. He also placed a small treat bag between us.

"Is someone sending you roses, Ms. Morgan?" Pierre asked.

"Yeah." I scrunched up my face and snatched my drink from the table. "Thank you for getting the drinks."

Pierre frowned and glanced at Estelle. His eyes grew wide. "What am I missing? Are flowers no longer an acceptable gift to show affection?"

"It isn't considered acceptable when the person sneaks into my apartment and leaves them on my bedside table. I have enough on my plate. I don't need a stalker."

Pierre straightened and his mouth dropped open. "Oh."

"Yeah." I took a sip of coffee and winced. The hot liquid burned my tongue and I cursed. Before Pierre turned away, I tapped the treat bag. "What's this?"

"Two cookies, compliments of Steve," Pierre answered.

"Steve?" Estelle asked, reaching over to lift the edge of the bag with one perfectly manicured nail.

"The barista," I answered, the familiar face and name finally clicking into place from my last visit.

"It's safe," Pierre said. "I watched him retrieve them from the display case. I figured if you didn't want them, we could—"

"Pffft." Estelle waved at him. "I never turn down chocolate chip cookies."

Pierre nodded and turned away to take up his post beside his vampire colleague.

Estelle pried one cookie out of the bag and took a

bite. She closed her eyes and moaned. "Fuck, this is good."

I smirked and tried my coffee's temperature again. "I can see that."

Estelle took another bite of the cookie before jerking her chin toward the bag where the other one waited. "You're not going to have one?"

"I prefer my calories in liquid form." I lifted my takeout cup.

Estelle shrugged and took another bite. "I've heard how you talk about tacos enough to know that's a lie."

I laughed and sank back into the booth. "You got me."

We sat in silence for a few moments while Estelle inhaled both cookies and I sipped my latte.

"Is Gregor ever going to let me pay for the last treatment?" I finally asked.

Estelle sighed and lowered the last of her cookie. "Honestly? He's probably saving your IOU card for a rainy day. Are you surprised?"

"No."

"Does this make things weird between you and me?"

"I don't think so."

"Good." She gave me a sympathetic smile before nodding at the café. "So you come here often enough for the barista to know your drink and give you free cookies?"

"Not really. I've only been here once." Kang had

bought me coffee, sat across the table from me, and told me I smelled nice.

"Your scent is intoxicating," he'd said while standing behind me. The rumble of his deep voice had caressed the sensitive skin on my neck while his hands had rested on my hips, the warmth of his touch spreading through me like a fire.

My cheeks heated.

Estelle's eyebrows shot up. She didn't miss much—she'd had a few lifetimes to learn how to read other people. "Must be some latté."

She glanced at her cup. She'd been too busy eating the cookies to try hers yet.

"It is nice. But enjoying my first coffee here got interrupted. It was all a part of a case." Wanting to jump Kang hadn't been, but I left that part out.

"Shame."

"Maybe it was for the best." I probably would've taken Kang home. Hell, I still wanted to take Kang home, but I also worked with him, and he was still keeping a secret from me. Maybe it was for the best that circumstances forced us to slow down a little.

We finished our drinks, waved at Steve as we left, and drove to my place. I said goodbye to Estelle and Antonia in the car and Pierre walked me to the front door of my apartment. We hadn't had much of a chance to talk privately tonight—he took his role as a guard seriously and I didn't want to mess with that.

"I'm glad to see you're doing well," I told him.

He tilted his head at me as if I said the oddest thing. "Thank you. It has been quite the adjustment, but I find I'm enjoying this new era."

We shared a smile.

I unlocked the door and Pierre held it open for me.

I stepped inside the apartment and turned to say goodbye. "I know it's a part of your job but thank you for guarding me tonight."

He nodded and released the door. "I will always protect you."

He turned to walk away, and the door whooshed shut and before my brain could process the words or muster any kind of response.

A chill ran along my spine—not because of Pierre's words—if anything, his words were kind and gave me warmth. No, the fear came from something else. It came from the knowledge that I had the power to control vampires, that I'd used that power on Pierre and he obviously still felt a piece of that connection. If Gregor ever discovered the extent of my magic, the vampires would go from protecting me to exterminating me.

NINE

The sun glared down on me, and I cursed. The sunglasses and pain killers did little to minimize the raging headache and unsettled stomach. I hadn't consumed enough alcohol last night to get super drunk, just enough to feel a little tipsy at the club and like garbage the next day. I might be young at heart, but my body was telling me I had definitely left my twenties behind.

I hadn't woken up to another rose, but I had been greeted with a hangover and a snarky twin who still wanted to pack me in bubble wrap and shove me in a vault. We'd argued. He'd called me stubborn, I'd called him a dick, and then we'd both left the apartment in a crappy mood.

"You look like shit, Morgan." Kang waved me through the crime scene checkpoint.

"Missed you, too, Kang." I stepped under the crime

scene tape. My world tilted, and I stumbled to the side.

Someone gripped my arm to steady me, and I looked up to find Kang standing impossibly close.

"Where the hell did you come from?" I asked. He moved fast.

His mouth twitched.

"Under the weather, Morgan?" Jacobs walked up to join us.

I grumbled and snatched my arm from Kang's grasp. "I don't look that bad. You two are just assholes."

Jacobs snickered.

"You never look bad," Kang said. "But you smell like a rundown alehouse." He wrinkled his nose.

"And you're wearing shades even though you just stepped into a shadowy forest," Jacobs added as if his commentary was needed or helpful.

"You used to be my favourite, Jacobs," I grumbled.

He laughed harder. "We all know Brandon is your favourite."

My mouth fell open. How did they know that? I didn't talk about the boys that much at work.

Kang leaned in. "We *are* detectives."

Speaking of detecting, I needed to tell Kang about the roses. Maybe he could weave some of that investigation magic and discover who was messing with me.

But now wasn't the time.

Maybe it was sheer foolishness not to mention the roses right away, but I could only manage so much at the moment and I needed to focus on the reason the detectives had called me here. I'd tell Kang later.

With an exasperated sigh, I walked past Kang and Jacobs to follow the trail to the crime scene. I'd tell him later.

"How could I forget you two are detectives?" I asked in a conversational tone. "You only mention it at every possible opportunity. Probably on your dating profiles."

One of them snorted behind me, but we walked along the path in silence. I didn't need directions.

The pressed gravel trail with the gentle slope ran through a dense evergreen forest with a few twists and turns. The stones crunched under our feet and the birds chirped merrily in the branches overhead. This section of park boasted a thick canopy, and despite the summer and lack of recent rain, pockets of dampness clung to the air along with the smell of moss heavy with dew.

My phone vibrated in my pocket. Peter's name flashed on the screen. I cursed and hit accept.

"Hey," I said. "I'm sorry. I meant to call you back."

"It's okay," Peter said. "You gave us quite a scare. I just wanted to follow up and make sure you were alive, and it wasn't some spectre texting back."

"I'm alive and well." I winced. That last part was a lie. My mental state was close to cracking.

"Glad to hear it. I have another case that's unlikely to resolve amicably, so I'll probably see you soon..."

"Sounds good," I said. He probably also wanted to ensure I wouldn't pull another disappearing act on the next raising I did for him. The client had likely asked a lot of questions he didn't have answers to. I couldn't promise that I wouldn't get sucked back into the veil again, so I didn't. Hopefully, Leviathan wouldn't pull the same trick twice. "Thanks for checking up on me."

"Any time."

We said goodbye and I hung up, still following the marked path to the crime scene while the detectives quietly followed.

"Who was that?" Kang asked.

I'd wondered if he'd break his silence first.

"Peter Schmidt."

Kang grumbled.

"It's not like that, Kang. He's a lawyer I often work with."

"I know who Peter is," Kang snapped.

Of course, he did. He probably ran a background check on him, too.

"I'm not upset about some guy calling you, Morgan," Kang continued while Jacobs remained suspiciously quiet. "I want to know what happened."

"Nothing."

"Lark." His tone had me turning around.

Jacobs flashed me a sympathetic smile and passed me, walking toward the crime scene to leave me alone with an angry Kang.

Traitor.

Kang had stopped walking and squeezed his eyes shut to take a deep breath. The sounds of the forest surrounded us, the whisper of a breeze through the leaves and the birds chattering away on the branches. Farther away, the babble of a fast-flowing river provided soothing background noise while crime scene analysts spoke in low voices and processed the scene.

"He said you scared him." Kang finally opened his eyes and broke the silence.

"Eavesdropping on my calls now?"

"Stop deflecting. You have the volume cranked and it was impossible not to hear."

I raised my eyebrows.

"What happened, Lark?" His expression softened.

"A spirit grabbed me after a routine raising and hauled me to the veil. Apparently, Leviathan wanted to have a word with me and felt that was the way to accomplish the task."

"Leviathan?"

"Yeah."

"The Lord of the Veil."

"That's the guy," I muttered.

"And you're alive?"

"Apparently."

"What did he want?" he asked.

It was my turn to sigh dramatically. "A date."

Kang's whole body went rigid, and fury streaked across his face. He balled his hands into fists. "What did you tell him?"

"Well, I wanted to say no. Actually, I did say no, but he persisted. I wasn't sure how well outright denying him a second time would go down. Men don't always take rejection well, and I was in difficult position of not wanting to die. I told him I'd think about it."

"I wasn't aware you were...acquainted." Kang pressed his lips together. "I know why I want to date you, and also that I have no claim on you. Yet. But why is the Lord of the Veil interested?"

"I'm still trying to figure that out. It may have to do with a lack of options, but I suspect he wants to use my magic somehow."

Kang flashed his teeth. "I don't like that you were in danger and some...thing...tried to use it to get a date."

"Going to place me in a padded room, Kang?"

"Would you let me?"

"Not a chance."

"How about I just handcuff you to a bed?" His gaze darkened. "My bed."

"Definitely not." Heat stirred within me, ready to answer that question in a completely different way. "You haven't even taken me out to dinner yet..."

He took a deep breath again and stepped forward. Starting at my shoulders, he ran his hands down my arms until he held my hands. "Will you let me know if you need help?"

"That I can definitely promise."

He squeezed my hands. "Are you okay?"

"Hungover as fuck and I only had like four or five drinks."

He waited.

"And kind of freaked out," I admitted. "Not just from getting pathetically hungover, but from Leviathan yeeting me from the living realm to proposition me."

Without a word, Kang pulled me in and wrapped his arms around me. With my face smushed into his neck, his subtle cologne surrounded me along with the warmth of his body.

What was happening right now? Had I entered a parallel universe? A few weeks ago, I never would've guessed I'd be standing here with Kang holding me. The same Kang who swore at me every time I arrived at a crime scene and called me a bone witch the first time we met.

The same Kang who'd quietly investigated my father's disappearance without being asked, who saved my life during our very first case together, who valued my input on spirit testimonies, and who caught me whenever I tripped and staggered at crime scenes.

Candace MacKinnon had been right.

Before the angry spirit had tried to kill me, she told me I didn't notice what was right in front of me. I never claimed to be the smart one in the family, but I wasn't a numbskull either. At least, not usually. I should've noticed Kang's qualities and feelings sooner.

I should've realized my own, too.

Luckily, I still had a chance to make it right.

"I can make this go away," Kang said. "I *will* make this go away." His chest rumbled with each word. "Just say yes and I'll handle it. I'll make him pay for every lost hour of sleep, every flinch, every fucking hesitation."

All the tension clinging to my shoulders left and I relaxed into his body. This hug felt like heaven. I wrapped my arms around him and let myself enjoy the feel of being held. The last thing I wanted was Kang going after the Lord of the Veil. But his words piqued my interest as much as they soothed me.

Curiosity really was my vice.

What the heck was Kang that he felt so confident he could go after Leviathan and succeed?

"Are you two going to make out or are we going to solve a murder?" Jacobs called out from the end of the path.

Kang reluctantly dropped his arms and I stepped away. Not knowing what to do or say, I smiled at Kang before turning to walk toward the crime scene.

A yellow strip of tape wrapped around a tree trunk marked the trail running off the main path. The small break in foliage was little more than a deer trail, and after pushing the ferns to the side, I picked my way carefully toward the sounds of talking.

People in white crime scene suits milled around a small clearing. The coroner would've had to clear the scene for me to enter, but the analysts often continued to work in the surrounding area for hours. I needed to ensure I stayed in the spots already processed.

Jacobs smirked at me as I passed and waggled his brows.

"Shut up," I muttered.

"Didn't say a thing." He linked his hands behind his back and whistled.

"You really are an asshole," Kang said.

"Takes one to know one," Jacobs called out.

Kang glared at his partner.

"What am I looking at?" I asked. We needed to change the topic before Kang killed Jacobs. I happened to like Jacobs, despite his teasing.

"Nothing good," Kang muttered.

"Is it ever?" I asked.

Kang grunted and looked away.

"This one is similar to the last one. Only fresher," Jacobs said. "Brace yourself."

Why he still bothered to issue warnings baffled me. No amount of bracing would help. These two didn't call me for tidy little scenes. They reserved me for the worst—the ones so disgusting and degraded that the help of a necromancer was their only shot at identifying the victim, murderer, or both. If I got called in by Jacobs or Kang, I knew it would be gruesome. I arrived as braced as I could ever be.

Maybe I could get another sympathy hug from Kang.

Officer Shaw stood at the end of the path, monitoring the active crime scene. I didn't know the officer well, but he didn't really provide much motivation to change that.

"Hello," I said as I walked past.

He frowned at me before turning away.

Okay, then...

Maybe under different circumstances I'd wonder what was up Shaw's ass, but death energy curled around me, dark and seducing. This might be a "fresher" scene compared to the last one, but the magic was weaker. Stale. The victim must've died months ago, and the body waited for me under the tarp, calling out to my magic.

I stopped at the edge of the small clearing and studied the white tarp that undoubtedly covered the found remains.

"Exactly how similar?" I asked.

"Very," Kang replied. He glanced at Officer Shaw briefly, his mouth turned down, before placing his hand on the small of my back to direct me toward the deceased. "Female victim. Single gunshot wound, body appears dumped."

"Who found her?" I approached the tarp.

Kang followed me while Jacobs hung back to speak with Shaw. "Jogger."

"On this trail?" I looked around. The body may have been dumped in a small clearing, but the path leading in and out of this area was little more than a glorified deer path.

"Trail running is a thing." He shrugged.

"A voluntary thing?" I blanched. That sounded like torture to me.

"Apparently." A smile tugged at the corners of his mouth. "Personally, I can think of better ways to exercise, but their story checks out so far."

"Better ways?" I raised an eyebrow.

"Focus, Lark. You have a job to do."

He was infuriating. "You know, working these scenes with you has convinced me of a few things." I knelt down and lifted the corner of the tarp.

"Oh yeah? What's that?" he asked. "I'm what's missing in your life?"

"Of course, but also, I don't think I'll ever own a dog or take up running."

Kang chuckled and shook his head. "You'll find death no matter where you go. You don't need either of those things to help you."

He had a point.

"Do you have a chicken?" I asked.

Jacobs cursed and spun on his heel. I'd spotted his car by the perimeter. He wouldn't take long to retrieve it. In the meantime, I stood in a crime scene alone with Kang. Sure, others milled around the edges, but the clearing felt very small all of a sudden, and my body still remembered how good it felt to be in his arms.

I looked away from his amused expression and studied the surroundings. There, a few feet into the trees grew a perfect ring of white mushrooms.

A fairy ring.

Myth claimed fairy rings acted as portals to the fairy realm. They could also strip fae of their glamour.

Fae could hear, see, and smell the dead.

Just like Kang...

My skin prickled with anticipation. This was my chance.

I made a show of continuing to search the forest before returning my attention to Kang. He stood perfectly still, watching me. Before I would've assumed his expression showed cold disinterest, but now I knew him better and I'd begun to catch his tightly controlled emotion. Kang wasn't disinterested at all. If anything, he held himself back from something he wanted very much.

Me.

Our gazes locked and we stared at each other while the breeze played with my hair and the analysts puttered around the edges of the crime scene. Neither of us said a word.

I swallowed, my mouth and throat suddenly dry.

"Got the chicken," Jacobs hollered out. "Did I miss anything?"

We both turned at the other detective's approach, and Jacob's smile faltered. Not sure what he saw, but it definitely startled him.

"I'll need you guys to stand over there." I pointed to the forest.

Kang following the direction of my pointed finger and frowned. "Why?"

"My magic has been a little wonky lately. Better safe than sorry." I pointed to the section of trees that had the fairy ring. "A foot or two into the trees over there should be fine."

Kang frowned even harder but complied. He walked over to the forest and stopped at the treeline. He bowed his head and studied the ground before glancing over his shoulder. "A fairy ring? Really?"

He didn't miss much.

"They say it will strip a fae of its glamour," I added, trying to keep my voice normal, but it came out higher pitched.

Kang barked out a laugh and stalked over to me. I froze like a deer caught in the headlights, watching his predatory advance. He stopped mere inches from me and leaned down to whisper in my ear. "I'm not fae, Lark."

My heart raced and warmth flooded my body at his proximity. Memories of dancing with him and how his body moved with mine raced through my mind.

He straightened and inhaled deeply. A smile tugged at his lips. "You still smell intoxicating."

Because I was an incredibly capable, strong-willed, grown-ass adult, I gaped at him and said nothing as he walked back to the fairy ring.

Jacobs snorted and walked over to join his partner. Kang turned so he faced me, his gaze sparkling with mischief. Keeping his attention on my face the entire time, he stepped backward until he stood in the center of the circle.

Nothing happened.

Dammit.

Guess that ruled out one possibility.

I clutched the chicken and turned to the deceased woman.

"Do we have to stay here?" Jacobs' stage-whispered behind me.

"She said better safe than sorry," Kang replied.

Ugh. Detectives.

I sighed and released the incoherent spirit to the veil. Luckily, this one hadn't received Levi's memo to abduct me, and I remained at the crime scene.

"Not good news, huh?" Jacobs leaned in and asked.

"Same as the last one," I said. "Mumbles and screams. No tongue. Dirty clothing. The killer must've anticipated the use of a necromancer. The only clear consistent thing they did was try to run away from me."

Jacobs cursed.

I turned to the ever-brooding Kang. "What are the chances this is just a coincidence and not connected to the other case?"

Kang just looked at me.

Of course they were connected. There might've been doubt before, but once this victim opened her mouth and wailed the same way, the margin of coincidence disappeared.

"How did you know?" I asked.

"Know what?" Kang's brows pinched down.

"How did you know this death was related to the last one? Even if the pathologist told you she died from a gunshot wound, you don't have any bullets to match, and these can't be the only dead women dumped in a forest during your career." Well, wasn't that a sad observation? I shuddered and mentally brushed away the unease.

Kang and Jacobs exchanged a look.

I leaned in and whispered, "Did you use your glamy sense of smell?"

Kang snorted. "My sense of smell is heightened, but it's not that powerful. Not like other glamies."

"Oh." Drat. I didn't know what to do with that information and I still didn't know how they anticipated these cases connecting. It had to be more than a hunch. More than a gut feeling—which was the lame excuse they'd given me the last time they linked two cases together before the evidence confirmed it.

One of the techs called out to Kang, and he stalked off to make someone else's life miserable with his glower.

"You're never going to guess, you know," Jacobs whispered.

"What?"

Jacobs jerked his chin in Kang's direction. "You're never going to guess."

Ah. He was talking about Kang's secret glamy identity. My brain was still stuck on the two mutilated bodies. These detectives took compartmentalizing to the next level.

"But you know," I said. "Why don't you tell me?"

Jacobs' smile widened. "What would be the fun in that?"

I sighed. I should've known he wouldn't be that accommodating. "That's just mean."

"I've had to spend the last six years playing referee while you two danced around each other," Jacobs said. "It's not mean. It's selfish. I deserve a little entertainment."

I wrapped my arms around my chest. "We didn't dance around each other."

Jacobs raised his eyebrows. "But you did dance *with* each other."

I sputtered.

Had Kang bragged about turning me into a puddle of goo on Spiral's dance floor? He didn't seem like the kiss-and-tell type. I narrowed my eyes at Jacobs.

No. Jacobs didn't find out from his partner. Kang wouldn't have said a thing to anyone, not even Jacobs. So how did he find out?

The detective stepped back and held up his hands. "As part of closing the case, we both had to submit statements in the final report. Kang left out the dancing, but to provide evidence to support his written testimony and the resolution of the case, we got a warrant and secured the security footage."

The security footage from Spiral...

Where Kang and I did our best vertical humping impression...

"Oh, god."

He nodded.

"How many people saw it?"

"The whole precinct before Kang shut it down. Most are too scared of Kang to say anything, especially after..." He glanced over at his partner. "Anyway. No one will say anything, but that didn't stop them from sharing the video."

I narrowed my eyes. What had Jacobs planned to say originally? Before Kang did what? Had Kang threatened every single one of his coworkers? I wanted to know, but I also had to let it go. Jacobs was a fucking vault. "Is that why Officer Shaw gave me that weird look?"

Jacobs turned toward the path. Neither of us had a clear view of where the officer in question stood by the check-in point, but that didn't stop either of us from trying.

"Nah," Jacobs said. "He's just weird."

Fair enough.

Kang walked back to where we stood and nodded at me. "I'll take you home."

I ignored the fluttering sensation in my heart and lifted my chin. "I drove."

"Then let me walk you to your car."

I couldn't argue with that. The sun had dipped past the treeline, creating long shadows that spread over the clearing. The quiet forest sent chills along my spine despite the heat of the day still warming my skin.

I saluted Jacobs as a goodbye, which earned me a dazzling smile and a nod.

Kang didn't speak as we ambled up the path and past Officer Shaw. When we finally reached my vehicle, he turned to me before I had a chance to say anything, and asked, "What night works for you?"

My mind faltered. So intent on figuring out how to segue to a discussion about the flowers, I mentally fumbled to switch gears, but once I did, I didn't have to ask what he meant. Our date. I wanted to start that date right now, but knew I'd have to wait.

"Let me check my schedule." I pulled my phone from my back pocket while my brain started functioning again. If I had to wait, I might as well try to use it to my advantage.

Kang shook his head.

"Unless you don't mind being double-booked with a cheating spouse death raising?" I lifted an eyebrow and flicked through my phone apps. "I mean, I could take you to a raising as a part of our date, if that's what you're into. No judgement."

I was lying about my schedule. Or at least misleading him. I already knew my work schedule. I needed to check the lunar calendar. I only knew of one other kind of glamy, other than fae, who could detect spirits the same way as Kang.

"How about two nights from now? Thursday?"

Kang's lips twitched, and he leaned forward to catch strands of my dark hair. He let them slip from his fingers. "I'm on call Thursday night."

"Aren't you on call every night?"

"Thursday night it is. I'll pick you up at six." He stepped back and turned to leave.

Dammit. I couldn't let him leave without telling him about the second rose. What if the stalker murdered me on my way home? Sure, my brother would avenge me, ruthlessly, but only after he figured out who did it and that would take time. And I'd already be dead.

Frankly, I didn't want to get killed by a rose-toting stalker. There was no need for me to keep this a secret and I didn't need to fight this battle alone. I'd take all the help I could get.

"Someone left me another rose," I blurted.

Kang froze. He slowly spun back toward me. "You asked me about a flower a few days ago, is this the same thing?"

I winced. "Someone left me a rose outside my apartment door. At least, I assumed it was for me.

There was no note. It wasn't my brother or his boyfriend messing with me. It wasn't from you or Gregor."

Kang narrowed his eyes.

Yeah, Kang had nothing to worry about with Gregor, but mentioning the master vampire's name probably wasn't the best idea, either. "And that's the flower I asked you about. I wasn't really worried..."

"Until?" Kang growled.

"The next day, I woke up to one on my bedside table."

Kang swore. Something dark flashed across his gaze, and he went impossibly still.

"I told my brother right away and he installed security cameras and he's been monitoring our block." I twisted my hands together. "And then the roses stopped. I didn't get one this morning. There were only the two, and—"

"Why are you just telling me this now?" Kang asked, his voice a deep rumble, like the thunder of an impending storm rolling in.

I swallowed before answering. "My brother—"

"I know exactly who and what your brother is, Lark," he snapped. "You still should've told me."

My stomach twisted, and Kang finally met my gaze. The sheer intensity flashing back had me staggering into my car. My butt hit the driver's side door and my breath rushed out of my lungs.

Kang followed, crowding my space. His hand shot up to cradle my cheek and jaw. Despite his whole body vibrating with rage, his touch was gentle, tender. "Just so we're clear. If anything ever threatens you, scares you, or makes you uncomfortable, I want to know."

"I—"

"I want to know, Lark. I want to know right away, even if it's me," he growled. "And I'll take care of it. Okay?"

"Okay," I said. Really, what else could I say to that?

He squeezed his eyes shut and took in a deep breath. His body relaxed a little and he stepped back, dropping his hand from my face. "Okay."

I swallowed again, still not quite sure how to respond. Honestly, if this had been a first date with a stranger, there'd be all sorts of red flags going up and I'd be finding a way out of the date.

But this was Kang.

He was a giant, walking red flag and instead of leaving me scared or worried, a different sort of reaction heated my body and left me breathless. Apparently, red was now my favourite colour.

"I'll see you at six." Kang spun around and stalked off toward the crime scene.

I climbed into my car on shaky legs and drove away, my mind still scrambled to catch up with what had just happened. Not only was Kang possessive as fuck and it turned me on, but Thursday night was a full moon. Kang hadn't hesitated to say yes to a date on that day. At all.

Either werewolves no longer had to shift on the full moon or he wasn't a werewolf.

But if he wasn't fae or a werewolf, what the hell was he?

ELEVEN

My phone flashed 2:00 am. Despite the summer month, a chill clung to the air. Exhaustion pulled at my eyelids, but weariness and adrenalin kept my heart pumping at a steady beat and my muscles tense.

I stood on the sidewalk just down the corner from Cathy's ground-level apartment. The spirit hadn't shown herself yet, but that didn't mean anything. I had shown up early in case the spirit did as well.

Death magic woven in the wind curled around me. I closed my eyes and reached out with my power. The well inside me vibrated, ready to burst forth. Tendrils of magic slipped along the pavement and caressed the outside of the building.

Nothing.

More nothing.

Wait.

My magic came into contact with the spirit and my skin tingled with energy and anticipation.

Was this the ghost or something else? Only one way to find out.

Keeping contact, I walked forward and opened my eyes. There, standing just around the corner, in plain sight of Cathy's living room window stood a spirit. Souls could choose to show themselves to drabs, but many either didn't care to or didn't have the energy of rage or wrongful death to materialize. I couldn't tell the difference. To me, spirits were always visible.

If Cathy could also see this spirit, though, either Cathy had magic of her own or this spirit wished to make her presence known.

Having met Cathy, option two seemed the most likely, which meant this wasn't just a spirit.

This was a ghost.

Ghosts were spirits fueled with extra magic due to the nature of their death. Not every soul who suffered traumatic death formed a ghost like this one or Bernie. There were often other factors involved, but a horrific death was generally a commonality.

This ghost had long straight hair cascading down her back, a petite stature and features consistent with East Asian ancestry. With high cheekbones and Cupid's bow lips, she would've been striking in life. In death, she had a hollowed-out, haunted appearance. A hazy outline of her clothes showed she'd worn jeans and a loose T-shirt at the time of her death.

They were ripped and blood-stained and hung off her lean frame.

The ghost turned to me, revealing a large gash down the other side of her face. The moment her gaze met mine, she jerked back and started to fade.

"No!" I reached out with my hand. "I just want to talk. I don't have your bones."

The ghost hesitated, but she didn't flee. Instead, she remained wavering on the corner of the intersection.

A car rolled by, and the woman in the passenger seat sneered at me but looked right past the ghost.

Huh.

Maybe not everyone could see her.

The ghost had dimmed in appearance. Instead of looking like a washed-out version of her former self, she'd become more of the glowing blue outline common to most spirits.

"I just want to talk," I repeated. This ghost was strong if she controlled her visibility to drabs.

"What's your name?" I asked, trying to keep her with me in the present.

The ghost swayed back and forth. "I...I don't know."

She had to be an older ghost if she no longer remembered her identity, but her clothes appeared contemporary, not dated. They looked like something I'd throw on to run to the store on my day off, hang out with friends, or go for a walk along the beach.

"Do you know what happened?" I asked. "Do you know why you're here?"

The ghost's appearance flickered. "A car. I remember a car, and pain, and...loss."

That would certainly explain the injuries. "Were you in the vehicle?"

"No...no, I was waiting. I was waiting for someone...someone I loved." She flickered again. "Mason."

I frowned. That wasn't a lot to go on, but at least I could search for pedestrian fatalities at this intersection.

"Where is she?" Cathy ran out of the building. "Where did she go?"

I jumped, surprised. Why the hell was my client running out on the street at two in the morning?

The ghost glanced between Cathy and me and disappeared. Just poof. Like that. Gone.

Cathy reached my side of the road and came to a stop a few feet away from me. "I saw you speaking to her before she disappeared. Did you get anything?" she asked, panting.

I swallowed my irritation. I probably would've gotten a lot more had Cathy not interrupted us but pointing that out right now wouldn't change anything.

Cathy waited expectantly.

"Not enough," I answered. "But I'll do some digging and find out more if you'd like."

Cathy bobbed her head. She'd already signed a contract to pay my hourly fee so she knew what she was getting into. At least financially. Denise made the money side of things very clear.

"If you had her bones, could you do more?"

I nodded. "I'll make some calls."

Cathy thanked me and returned to the building. Once she was out of sight, I pulled out my phone and dialled Kang.

"What?" His tone was raspy, his voice clipped. He sounded both pissed off and tired—so basically, he sounded like his normal self. He definitely didn't sound surprised to get a call from me at two in the morning.

Nor was I shocked he answered the phone despite the time. He worked hours just as ridiculous as mine. "Your phone manners are atrocious."

"I'm in the middle of a case, Lark," he said, his voice dropped lower. "You can teach me manners later."

A smile tugged on my lips. "I bet you'd like that."

"Did you phone to flirt with me or is there another reason for your call?"

"First of all, if you think that's flirting, I have more than manners to teach you, but second, yes. I'm calling for a different reason. Can you pull up car accidents that occurred at a specific intersection that resulted in the fatality of a young, East Asian woman? A man named Mason may have been involved and it may have occurred on the twentieth of the month. Probably at 2 am."

"That's oddly specific."

"It's for a client." I rambled off the street names of the intersection.

"I can't access records without just cause or a case number."

"Make one then. This is in the public's best interest. There's a disproportionately higher incidence of accidents occurring at this location, and I believe a ghost is responsible."

"You're there right now?" he asked.

"Yes."

"And your beliefs are based on what?" He sighed, loudly. "No. Don't answer that. Let me guess. You've already located the ghost and spoken with her. Probably alone."

"I guess that's why you're the detective."

"Do you have her bones?"

"No."

Kang swore, knowing that meant an increased risk. "Did you get her name?"

"Also no, that's why I need your help."

Kang swore again.

"Does that mean you'll do it?"

"Of course, I'll do it," he said before hanging up on me.

TWELVE

After a regular day at work, no roses, no detectives, no vampires or ghosts, I walked into my apartment and into the middle of an argument. Maggie shot from the living room and wound around my feet, pressing her white fluffy fur into my leather-covered legs. A few feet away, Logan and Brandon faced each other in the hallway leading to the living room, faces red, hands balled into fists and tense shoulders.

"Whoa. What's going on here?" These two rarely fought unless the last taco was involved.

Brandon broke eye contact first. "You need to talk some sense into your brother."

"Agreed. But just so we're on the same page, what am I trying to ram through his thick skull this time?" I mean, there were plenty of things.

"I'm right here," Logan huffed. He placed a hand

on his hip, looking the exact opposite of threatening. He was a lethal assassin for Victoria's underground glamies, but he certainly didn't look it right now.

Brandon ignored Logan's comment and turned to me, pushing his curls from his face. He needed a haircut. "We were discussing our living arrangements."

"Oh."

I adored living with my brother and while Brandon technically had his own place, he was over often enough that I considered him my third roommate and second brother. Honestly, sometimes I loved him more.

Logan couldn't move out. I'd be all alone.

I winced and cursed myself. What an incredibly selfish thought.

"See?" Logan waved his hand at my face. "You upset her."

Brandon sighed and walked over to gather my hands. "I love your brother and want to officially move in with him."

I nodded and bit my lip. "You already kind of live with him here."

"Not technically, though," Brandon said.

"But you could," I said. "Make it technical...or official...or whatever." I was grasping at straws, and I really needed to let Logan and Brandon go. I wasn't their responsibility.

"I was proposing we move out and find a bigger place."

"Oh." I squeezed my eyes shut and mentally kicked

myself. *Grow up, Lark.* "I love both of you and want you to do whatever will make you happy."

"Ugh." Brandon shook my hands before dropping them. "I was suggesting we all move out, Lark." He waved his finger in a circle to point at me, Logan and then himself. "All three of us. We should move out and find a bigger place. I won't be paying separate rent for a place I don't use and you two no longer have to save for your mom's medical treatments. Plus, there's the whole creepy flower thing. Sometimes avoidance is the best defense."

Logan barked out a laugh and mumbled, "Bullshit," under his breath.

I narrowed my eyes.

Logan grunted. "I disagree. Respectfully. I think we should let this rose-fucker try to sneak in again so I can deal with him. As for the living arrangement, I was saying we shouldn't give up an already great apartment when he could just let his go and move in here. We've got a great landlord and our rent is actually reasonable."

"Oh, you guys." I let out a long, quivering breath. "Why did you have to fucking scare me like that?"

Brandon laughed and pulled me into a hug, squishing my face into his solid chest. "Did you actually think we'd leave you alone, Sunshine? You're stuck with us, babe."

"At least until you find someone of your own who will put up with your shit," Logan answered.

"That comment is why I love Brandon more than you," I mumbled into Brandon's sweater, blinking away unshed tears. How dare my eyes prickle right now. I was a badass necromancer.

I pulled away from Brandon and winked at Logan so he'd know I was just joking. Sort of. He shook his head while Brandon, the traitor, chuckled.

Normally, my knee-jerk reaction to Logan's comment would be to throw my upcoming date in his face, but Kang was different. Everything felt so fragile but also monumental. Like I'd arrived at a crossroad and one way led to pure happiness and the other to utter ruin.

I didn't want anything to mess up this date.

But what if the date was awful?

Oh god.

What if I had to keep seeing him after the bad date?

Sure, I could be professional, but that didn't mean I wouldn't feel awkward.

Oh god.

What if it was great? What if he knocked me off my feet and I never managed to stand up again without him?

"Why does it look like you just tried to do some mental math?" my brother asked.

"It's nothing."

Both men perked up.

Ugh. Definitely not the right choice of words.

My cell phone vibrated in my pocket. I held up my finger to delay the inquisition and pulled my phone free. Kang's name appeared on the screen.

"Saved by the bell," Brandon muttered.

"I loved that show," I said absently. Growing up, we'd watch the reruns on repeat all the time.

The boys shared a look and spoke in unison. "Zach."

Brandon lightly whacked Logan's chest and nodded in the living room's direction. Logan grinned and they walked away to give me some privacy.

They better never leave me. I'd be ruined.

I accepted the call. "Hello?"

"We identified the body from the second scene," Kang said as a greeting. "Her name is Amelia Mills."

"And you're calling me to celebrate?"

Kang grunted. "No. The deceased lived around the block from you. We're going to search her apartment. Would you like to come along?"

I didn't have to think about it. Of course, I wanted to go. "I love it when you talk dirty to me."

Kang didn't respond right away. I could just picture him, standing off to the side of some crime scene frowning at his phone.

"Oh, Lark," Kang practically purred into the phone. "It looks like I have some things to teach you, too."

THIRTEEN

Kang and Jacobs met me outside the tall apartment building. I'd walked past this place with Logan and Brandon countless times. Had I seen the victim before? Smiled and waved?

I snorted. Who was I kidding? I'd never smile or wave at a stranger. If anything, I'd give the typical closed-mouth half-smile with a chin lift—the acceptably awkward Canadian greeting reserved for accidentally making eye contact with a stranger.

The building looked like any of the others in the area. As though someone had taken a large rectangular block from a giant's playset and set it down in nature, the structure sat there, bold, and completely at odds with the mountain-view behind it. The off-white paint covering the stucco siding hadn't aged well, and a green film had begun to grow on one side.

A man waited on the other side of the glass door and straightened as we approached. Before Kang could knock, the man opened the door and stood to the side to let us in. Tall and lean, he looked like he'd snap in a strong gust of wind. "I'm Tom, the building manager."

Jacobs showed Tom the warrant to search the premises. "My name is Detective Jacobs. We spoke on the phone." He jerked his chin in Kang's direction, then mine. "This is my partner Detective Kang and our consultant, Ms. Morgan."

Tom nodded at each of us and offered his hand. After we took turns shaking his hand, he asked, "Elevator or stairs?"

"Stairs," all three of us responded.

Tom rocked back on his heels and his eyes widened. He swallowed and nodded, waving his hand to a door on his right. No one spoke as we made our way to the second floor. Guess there was little need for idle chit-chat during a police investigation.

The apartment building had that universal smell of any building from the 70s in the Pacific Northwest. A mixture of stale cigarette smoke, dirt, sweat and mould. It wasn't strong enough to be unpleasant, but if someone wanted to bottle "old apartment" as a scent, this would be it.

"Here we go. Apartment 207." Tom knocked on the door and then turned to us. His black hair didn't have any gray, but the dark bags under his eyes made him appear older than he probably was. "She had a roommate. Odette. Her sister, I believe."

"When was the last time you accessed this apartment?" Jacobs asked.

The building manager frowned and stood by the door for the longest three seconds of my life.

"About three weeks ago?" he finally answered. "I'd have to check my notes. Odette had a problem with the circuit breaker. Amelia was already missing for about three months by then. I remember because Odette broke down and cried a few times while I was fixing the electrical panel."

Kang nodded. "Thank you for that information. We'll need you to stay outside to reduce contamination in case this is a crime scene."

Tom nodded, unlocked the door, and stepped back. After calling out to announce themselves, Kang entered the apartment first, then Jacobs. Lucky me followed after them and death magic hit me in the face instantly upon entering.

There was a dead body in the apartment.

Keeping my mouth shut, I stood in the entry way and waited for Tom to give us some privacy. I didn't need either of the detectives to tell me to keep my hands to myself. I'd been in enough of their crime scenes to know better than to touch anything. Tom reached forward, said goodbye, and closed the door, leaving the three of us in the apartment with the dead body while he went on with his night.

Finally. I drew in a deep breath while the death magic continued to buzz around me. "Ugh...guys?"

Kang held up his hand and drew his service firearm.

"We know," Jacobs said. "We smell it."

What the fuck did he mean by that? I couldn't smell a thing. The apartment had a synthetic fresh laundry smell. I probably had the same plugin at one time.

"Stay here." Kang pointed to where I stood near the entrance by the closet. A pair of black heels lay on the floor as if recently kicked off after a night out. I'd done the same thing countless times.

The wood flooring creaked as Kang and Jacobs moved through the rooms to clear the apartment.

"Jacobs," Kang called out. "You need to see this."

I drifted forward to peer around the corner, but I couldn't see Kang.

Jacobs cursed and ice prickled my spine. My magical senses hadn't led me astray. Someone had died here recently. But if I couldn't smell the body, how did Kang and Jacobs?

Kang walked around the corner and froze. In a blink of an eye, he had his firearm pointed at me.

What the hell?

"Victoria Police," Kang called out. "Drop it."

An arm wrapped around my shoulders and something cold pressed to my temple.

"I don't think so," an unfamiliar male voice spoke

near my ear. His breath fanned my hair. His shirt smelled like he'd pulled it straight from a mail order bag and hadn't washed it before putting it on, and his skin smelled like mild soap.

My heart stopped a beat. A gun. A stranger had a gun pressed to my head. Had he been hiding in the closet when we entered the apartment?

Kang's face contorted with rage. "If you step away from her right now, you'll live."

As much as I appreciated his sentiment, I hadn't plodded along the last six years content to remain defenceless and hope someone else would save me if I ever got into a predicament like this again. I'd had a gun pointed at me before. The last time, I'd felt helpless. This time, I'd save myself.

I gathered my magic around me. The death had been recent, and the spirit answered my call without a spell or drop of blood.

Odette was here and she was pissed.

With my breath caught in my throat, I used my magic to drive Odette's soul into the man's mind. He howled and reared back. My heart beat so frantically, it might self-destruct. I slammed my elbow into the man's ribs. He howled and doubled over, swinging at empty air. I ducked out of his control and stepped to the side.

My magic connected with his soul.

You could wrench it from him, my power whispered. *You could destroy him.*

My fingers tingled and prickling warmth spread

through my limbs. My magic gripped his soul, ready to rip it from his body at my command. Before I had a chance to tell my own thoughts to go to hell, or act on the ideas, Kang barrelled into the man, tackling him to the ground.

"Victoria PD." Jacobs somehow appeared from the other direction, his firearm trained on my would-be killer. "Stay down," he yelled. "Stay down or I'll shoot."

The click of handcuffs drew my attention back to the man writhing on the floor. Somehow, in the short time I'd looked away, Kang had disarmed the man, rolled him on his stomach and handcuffed his wrists together behind his back.

With a feral snarl, Kang leapt to his feet and spun to face me. His wild gaze raked my body. He stepped forward and he hesitated. What had he planned to do? To say?

"She's okay, Connor," Jacobs said.

That was debatable. My mind reeled and not just because I'd been held at gunpoint. My magic had wanted to rip the man's soul from his body. Why? Could I even do that? Or had Odette's spirit somehow boost my power?

Kang rocked back on his heels and after he took another second to scan me, his shoulders relaxed. He took a deep shuddering breath in. "Fuck, Lark. That took ten years off my life."

"You're practically geriatric now."

"Don't." He squeezed his eyes shut, his body vibrated. "Don't joke right now."

Fair enough. Adrenaline still thrashed through my body, leaving me shaky. With Kang standing off to the side, I finally got a good look at the man. Of average build and wearing all black, he continued to scream and convulse on the floor.

Jacobs looked up from his target. "What the fuck did you do to him?"

I shrugged. "Odette was pissed. I gave her some power for payback."

The detectives gaped at me.

With a shudder, the man went limp on the ground. He lay there as we stared down at him, his chest rising ever so slightly.

Odette's spirit rose from his body. She hovered in front of me and pulsed brightly before streaking away.

"He's still alive?" I asked, though I knew he had to be. Not only did I see his chest moving a moment ago, I'd never heard of a spirit directly killing a human.

Now, making someone go mad or driving them to hurt themselves or others? Yes, that was definitely within the skill set of an angry spirit.

Kang knelt and checked his pulse. "He's alive... Unfortunately."

I tsked. "So vicious."

"He killed a woman and held a gun to your head, Lark," Kang snapped. "Don't expect me to have compassion for someone who deserves none."

"So, it's Odette?" I had already assumed as much, but spirits didn't wear name tags.

"Yes." Jacobs sat down on a dining room chair. "Single bullet wound to the head. Execution style."

"Could this be the guy?" I asked. "For the other murders?"

"Doesn't feel right," Kang said.

Rather ominous. What did that even mean?

"He could be." Jacobs scratched his chin. "But it's also possible he knows the killer and was helping with clean up."

Kang stayed kneeling beside the man and searched his pockets. If this guy was a professional, Kang wouldn't find much.

My stomach twisted. "Somehow the latter seems worse. I would do a lot for my bestie, but I'd draw the line at murder."

Kang snorted and stood from where he'd crouched near the unknown man. "Lark. We both know you'd kill and then some to protect your brother and Brandon. But this doesn't feel like a sibling or bestie rage-killing."

"How so?"

"Too clean." Kang and Jacobs answered in unison.

"Killer for hire?" I asked. "I've never met an assassin before." Other than my brother, of course.

"Sure you have," Jacobs said.

I blinked at him. Shit. Did he know about Logan, too? Had Kang told him?

Jacobs leaned in. "You've met them, you just didn't know they were assassins." He turned to Kang. "Did you find anything on him?"

Phew. Thank you Jacobs for changing the subject. I didn't relish discussing my potential knowledge of assassins. I tried not to release all the pent-up air from my lungs.

Kang glanced over and smirked. He said he knew who and *what* my brother was. How much did he know and how did he find out?

Before I could ponder the answers to those questions, Kang held out a card. "Just this."

He flicked it back and forth so we could inspect both sides. One side of the parchment-coloured card was blank, and the other side had a seven-digit number, starting with three very familiar numbers.

"Phone number?" I asked.

"That's a B.C. area code if it is," Jacobs nodded. "Local."

"Let's find out." Kang pulled out a black flip phone, presumably a burner and punched the numbers. He turned on the speaker phone and we huddled around, waiting to see if anyone would pick up.

"Spiral," a familiar voice spoke through the phone.

I stiffened. Jacobs raised both blond eyebrows. Kang's expression remained blank and devoid of emotion.

Instead of saying anything, Kang hung up and exchanged a look with Jacobs.

"That was Grant, the club owner at Spiral." I pointed at Kang's burner.

"The same fuckstick who tried to barter for a dance with you," Kang spoke with clipped words.

Now wasn't the time to point out that Grant hadn't simply tried, he'd succeeded.

And I'd made him pay for the audacity.

"I saw him the other day. Apparently, my dancing skills weren't as much of a deterrent as I'd originally hoped," I said.

Kang narrowed his eyes at me.

"We could use that." I shrugged.

Kang stilled and violent energy vibrated from him. Darkness flashed across his gaze. I winced and took a step back.

Jacobs coughed into his sleeve and walked around the corner, presumably where Odette's body lay.

"Lark," Kang started.

"Yes?"

"Please stay away from that club," he said. "Let us handle this."

"Are you ordering me?" Technically, he said please and phrased it as a request, but his tone and body language suggested something more demanding.

"Of course, not." He took a deep breath and rolled his shoulders back "You're an intelligent, independent woman. I'm merely pointing out Grant is now a suspect in three homicides and it's not safe to go to his club when he's shown particular interest in you." He added a soft smile as if it would somehow camouflage his obvious tactics of using flattery to get his way.

I pointed at him. "You're infuriating."

He reached out with quick reflexes and grabbed my hand. He pulled me forward to press my hand to his chest. His heart was beating really hard, and really quickly. "I don't like the idea of you becoming the fourth victim. Please be careful," he said, his voice low and growly.

Damn. It was hard to argue with him like this. When he let me peek behind that tough, grumpy exterior, I wanted to do really bad things despite my would-be assassin lying on the floor a few feet away and the sound of sirens growing louder with each heartbeat. Jacobs must've called it in while he was in the other room.

"Okay," I said. He made excellent points, and I had no plans to argue with him.

Kang cleared his throat and dropped my hand. "Also, I meant to tell you earlier. I have some information on that case you wanted me to open."

Case? Right now, I was trying to figure out how to tactfully reschedule our date to right now so I could take him home. Sure, I probably needed therapy for having a gun pressed to my head, but I couldn't think of anything more therapeutic right now than letting Kang do things to my body to keep my mind off what had just happened. And what could've happened had things gone the other way.

I shivered.

"Morgan?" Kang watched me, his dark gaze scanning my face.

"What case?"

"The ghost on the street corner," he said.

My mind scrambled and then the haunting image of the spirit on the road flashed in my mind.

Right.

"The ghost case? You found her?"

"Yeah. Sad story. Lily Zheng was struck by a car at that intersection four years ago."

Only four years ago and she'd already forgotten her name? That didn't quite fit. "And you're sure it's her?"

"You didn't give me a lot of standard search parameters to go on besides 'young East Asian.' The demographics of the community and traffic at that intersection meant my search yielded a lot of victims who fit the criteria. But Lily is the first one in a string of accidents, had a boyfriend named Mason and the time of death was estimated at around two in the morning."

"How far back did you go?"

"Fifty years."

He knew me well. Those were the search parameters I would've asked for.

"No one else fits the description, location, TOD, and cause of death before Lily. I can send you a picture of her."

I nodded. His reasoning was sound. "Was the driver charged?"

"Hit and run."

I swore.

"I know. It gets worse. She was waiting on the corner for her boyfriend Mason to pick her up. He never showed. But witnesses claim to have seen a black Honda Civic leave the scene."

"Common enough car."

"Same make, model and colour as the boyfriend's car. The investigators suspected either the boyfriend or one of his parents, but they couldn't prove it. The car had been reported stolen the night before and they never recovered it."

"Wow."

"She was four months pregnant."

I squeezed my eyes shut. I'd been in the business long enough to know life was unfair and cruel, but stories like this still stabbed at my heart.

"If it's her, it certainly explains the rage and the power she demonstrated."

"She's buried at Royal Oak Burial Park under her Chinese name," Kang said. "Zheng Mei Hua."

His phone buzzed and he glanced at the scene. "The team is here. Do you want to wait outside? An independent investigator will have to take your statement before you can leave."

I nodded and turned to leave.

"I can come with you," Kang offered.

"And hold my hand?"

"If you want."

"I'll be okay," I lied.

Kang hesitated.

"You have a job to do," I told him. "I'm fine and if that changes, I'll call."

Kang clamped his mouth shut and jerked his head up and down in a tense nod that told me two things— he didn't believe me when I said I was fine, and he didn't like leaving me alone.

I gave him what I hoped would be a reassuring smile and tried to walk calmly out of the apartment.

Kang growled behind me.

"Let her go," Jacobs said. "You heard her..."

I closed the door on the rest of the conversation and backtracked my way through the building while first responders rushed past me.

Taking a deep breath, filled with old apartment air, I focused on placing one foot in front of the other down the hallway and stairs. With my breathing under control, I paused in the lobby and pulled out my phone. I found Cathy's contact information and dialled her number. I could at least knock one thing from my list while I waited to give my statement. It would help keep my mind distracted. My hands still shook, but focusing on a simple, normal task helped.

"Hello?" Cathy answered.

"Hi, Cathy, this is Lark Morgan."

"Oh...oh, hello."

"Does the name Lily Zheng mean anything to you?"

Silence answered me.

I waited.

"No. Should it?"

"I believe that is the identity of the woman who is haunting the corner outside your apartment."

"Oh..." she repeated. "You're very fast."

"I had some assistance."

"Do you have enough to help her rest now?" Cathy's voice trembled.

"No. I still need her bones and a sacrifice to do that."

"And I guess it will take a while to locate her remains. There are a lot of cemeteries, and some families are very private about details."

"They can be, but that won't be an issue. She was buried under her Chinese name—Zheng Mei Hua at Royal Oak."

More silence.

I didn't know Cathy well. Hell, I didn't know her at all besides how she promptly paid the invoice sent to her and her obsession with this ghost. Was there something else I was missing?

"How would you like to proceed? I can go by in the next night or two if you'd like for me to help her to the veil."

"Oh, ah yes. Yes, that will work. Please continue and keep me informed," Cathy said in a rush of words.

I said goodbye and hung up. Something wasn't quite right about this case. I liked to believe in humanity's possible redemption, but why would a single woman care so much about a ghost to foot the bill to see her at rest?

Maybe I'd become too cynical, but it just seemed odd.

CHAPTER

FOURTEEN

After an independent investigator gently took my statement and contact information, I left the active crime scene. I wouldn't be charged for necromancer assault as I clearly acted in self-defence, the two detectives backed my statement, and the man had a gun at the scene of a murder. Though VicPD would have to wait for ballistics results and other corroborating evidence, dollars to donuts, the bullet used to kill Odette would match the assassin's gun and ammunition.

I was just glad Kang didn't have to shoot anyone. In our last case, he'd fired his service firearm, saving a cheating woman from her spirit-possessed partner. But for all Kang's gruff exterior, taking that shot had cut him deeply.

I pushed thoughts of Kang from my mind and relaxed into the passenger seat. Estelle had called me to go out with her again, and I'd happily agreed. I needed a distraction. The alternative meant sitting alone in my apartment to overthink how I'd had a gun to my head and how today's events could've gone completely different. My hands still shook.

"We're here," Estelle announced.

I looked out the town car's window and froze. The familiar neon light lit up the interior of the vehicle. I shot my hand out and grabbed Estelle's forearm without thinking. She had one jeweled high heel already on the pavement, ready to gracefully emerge from the car.

Instead of biting my hand off, Estelle merely turned toward me and raised an eyebrow.

"I can't go in there," I said. I should've asked where we were headed when I got into the car.

Estelle frowned. "We were here the other night."

"Yeah, but..." I looked away and removed my hand from Estelle's arm. I couldn't dish details about Kang and Jacob's ongoing investigation, and telling Estelle a man told me not to go to the club sounded lame, even to me.

Despite what Kang might think, I didn't have a death wish. I agreed to stay away from Grant's club because I agreed with Kang. He was looking out for me, not trying to control me and I appreciated the difference.

Estelle waited patiently, one leg still out of the car, her hand propping the door open.

I sighed. I was with the human servant to the Master Vampire of Victoria, and two vampire guards from his inner circle—Antonia and Pierre. Gregor wouldn't let anything happen to Estelle, but second to that, I was an asset to him as well. He wouldn't risk my safety, either.

"Never mind," I mumbled. I would be safe with Estelle.

"That's my girl." Estelle winked and slipped from the town car.

Pierre opened my door and held out his hand to help me from my seat. I placed my hand in his smooth, cold palm, and he gently lifted. I flashed him a smile in thanks and followed Estelle into the club.

The entrance led to a lobby with a cashier to take payments for the cover and a booth of sorts to collect coats. We walked past all of that without stopping and through another bouncer-lined entrance.

We made our way to a private booth with a sign marked reserved and Estelle slid onto the leather seat on one side while I mirrored her actions on the other. Antonia and Pierre stood at the end of the table, awaiting orders, and giving me a powerful sense of déjà vu.

"Does this club frighten you, Lark?" Estelle cocked her head.

"No, of course not."

Estelle nodded at Pierre, and he disappeared into

J. C. MCKENZIE

the throng of people, presumably to get us drinks. Antonia turned her back to us to survey the club.

"Then what does scare you, Lark?" Estelle asked, a mischievous twinkle in her gaze.

"The Lord of the Veil," I answered immediately. "I'm not sure which of the many cautionary bedtime stories were scarier—those involving Leviathan or the ones with barghests."

"What's a barghest?" Estelle's forehead wrinkled adorably when she frowned.

"I thought you were supposed to be the old and knowledgeable one."

Estelle scoffed and leaned back in her seat. The leather creaked. The strobe lights danced along her exposed skin. Pierre returned in record time with two martinis and slid them across the table's surface.

"Thank you," I said.

"Of course, *ma belle.*" Pierre winked and turned around to stand guard with Antonia.

"Barghests are nasty necromancer-munching monsters," I explained.

Estelle jerked back. "Well, that sounds horrific." She paused. "That's not what I meant, though, when I asked what scared you." Estelle sipped at her martini. "This boogeyman from the veil and the barghests, those are fearsome things that would scare anyone. What I want to know is what you truly fear in this life."

"Geez, Estelle. Getting pretty deep straight away and I haven't even had one drink." Did she plan to

144

relay the information to Gregor? Use it against me? As much as I wanted Estelle as a friend, I couldn't forget where her loyalties lay.

Estelle laughed and took another sip.

I reached out and grabbed my own drink. The cool liquor coated my tongue with a delicious balance of sweet and sour. A crantini, one of my favourites.

"I'm scared of being left," I finally answered after a few more sips. This sad truth wouldn't give Gregor any more power over me if the information got back to him. Gregor already knew I'd do anything for my family, and I loved them most in the world.

Estelle placed her glass down. "Being left alone?"

"I guess. I can handle being alone if it's by choice and temporary. I worry about being left by those I love. I'm worried my mother will succumb to her illness and leave me. I'm worried my brother will get his own place with his boyfriend and they'll leave me, too. And yes, I know how incredibly selfish that sounds. And how needy." I sipped more of my martini. "I'm worried they'll leave, just like my dad left."

"Ah." Estelle's expression softened. "Now who's getting deep?"

I scrunched up my nose and took another sip. "You asked."

Estelle nodded. "And it turns out you have some unresolved daddy issues."

I stiffened. She wasn't wrong, but I didn't like my pain being boiled down to that one, over-used expression. My hand drifted to my neck involuntarily, seeking to touch the cold metal of my pendant necklace—the only real thing other than DNA I had left from my father. He and my brother had identical necklaces to mine.

Estelle held up her hand in a silent apology. "Thank you for sharing this with me. There's no judgement here, Lark. Not from me. I think a lot of people share the same fear."

"Do you?"

Estelle sighed again and looked away. "I'm practically immortal. While I might've feared being left in the past, I have said so many goodbyes over my lifetime that I'm desensitized to the pain of loss. I have had people leave me since I took my first sip of blood. In a way, it's me who is leaving them behind. Like I'll leave you. It's a bittersweet pain, but one I'm accustomed to. One I will gladly continue to bear because the alternative would be much, much worse."

"Then what do you fear?"

"I fear losing my humanity. I fear when my time finally does come, I'll have nothing to show for it, nothing to justify the gift of time I was given except an empty shell. I will have left no legacy."

She took a sip of her martini to punctuate her confession. Silence filled the booth, though the bass of the music continued to thump, and people partied all around us.

"Well, shit." I held up my glass. "I didn't realize we were competing, but congratulations. I think you win."

Estelle shook her head and a small laugh escaped. She held up her glass and we clinked the rims together.

"To friendship," Estelle said.

"To friendship." I drank more of my martini, enjoying the buzz in my head and the warmth in my belly. "Are we going to share sad stories all night or are we going to dance?"

Estelle laughed, her gaze alight with more mischief. "As long as you promise not to stomp on my feet, we're dancing." Estelle slid from the booth and pushed Antonia to the side. I followed suit, minus man-handling Pierre, and joined Estelle on the dance floor.

Unease prickled my spine, and I looked up. Grant stood on the balcony overlooking the dance floor, his arms folded over his shirt, one hand holding a takeaway coffee cup. I could be looking at a serial killer and here I was, dangling myself like a carrot in front of a rabid bunny. Grant studied me openly, but when my gaze met his, he nodded and walked away.

Maybe he wasn't a killer. Maybe he wasn't hunting tonight. Or maybe, my entourage of powerful vampires and a human servant acted as enough of a shield against whatever interest he had in me.

Estelle grabbed my hands and pulled me in to bounce around to the current song. I didn't mind. I planned to stick to the human servant's side all night.

But what would happen once I no longer had my

powerful friends beside me? I hadn't thought that part through, but before concern set in, someone bumped into me. I glanced over my shoulder and spotted blonde hair swaying to the beat. "Denise?"

My friend looked over her shoulder and her eyes widened. "Lark?"

We hugged in the middle of the dance floor with the throng of people around us and the heavy bass thudding. Denise's normally full, bouncy blond hair hung limply from the heat of the room. She wore a short leather skirt, black lace stockings and a matching black lace shirt that showed off her black bra underneath and magnificent breasts. She smelled of floral perfume and beer.

Maybe I should slow down on the martinis. I'd only had one so far and I was already hugging. I wasn't normally a hugging person.

I drew back and returned Denise's smile. Two men behind her leered over her shoulder. They looked like slimy twins with hair gelled back with way too much product, hollow cheekbones and gazes that lingered a little too long on Denise's ass and my chest.

"This is Stanley and Cooper." She jerked her thumb over her shoulder. "Boys, this is my co-worker and friend, Lark."

I managed a nod and a smile, but it probably looked like a grimace because both of them scowled.

"This is Estelle." I tilted my head in the human

servant's direction. I had to shout a little over the music. "Estelle, this is Denise."

"Charmed," Estelle said. Her smooth voice flowed easily. She didn't sound like a shrill harpy like me.

"Can I join you guys?" Denise asked.

"Of course," Estelle answered before I had a chance.

I would've told her to lose the losers first, but I'd never been accused of tact.

Denise beamed at Estelle and then turned to say something to the two men behind her. Their scowls deepened and with dark looks flung our way, they stalked off into the gyrating mass of partiers.

"Where are they going?" I asked.

Denise lifted a brow and started swaying to the beat again. "Did you want me to call them back?"

"God, no."

Denise giggled and continued to move to the music. "I was getting tired of the twins anyway."

"You have awful taste," I said.

"They're hot." She announced this like it explained everything.

They might have classically attractive features, but they were most definitely not hot. Instead of arguing with Denise, I shrugged and picked up dancing again. I tried to shake off the sense of dread gnawing at my spine. I danced in a club owned by a potential serial killer, but I faced other dangers as well.

Denise was my friend, true, but she was also my

supervisor at work and tasked with keeping Raisers accredited. If she ever found out I did illegal raisings for the Master Vampire of Victoria, my actions would place her in a difficult position. She was duty bound to report me, and if she didn't and someone discovered she lied for me, she'd also lose her licence.

I tried to dance off the ill-ease, my work friend on one side, my vampire servant friend on the other. Estelle wouldn't reveal my involvement with Gregor. Neither of them wanted my affiliation well known because I could be used against Gregor.

Deep breath, Lark. It's going to be okay.

The bass kept pounding, and I kept swaying, but a headache began to bloom behind my eyes.

I was about to lean over to Estelle and call it an early night when my phone vibrated in my pocket. I pulled out the device and read the text message on the screen.

"I have to go," I shouted over the music.

"What?"

"I have to go." I waved my phone at Denise and Estelle.

Estelle smiled and nodded. She glanced over at Pierre and tilted her head.

Denise's gaze flicked between the three of us and her mouth turned down in a pout.

"It's Kang."

Denise perked up at that. Her body smacked into mine, all hot and sweaty, without warning and as fast as she trapped me in her toned arms, she released me and stepped back. She circled her finger at the three of us. "We should do this again."

"Yeah, totally." I waved goodbye and walked over to the edge of the dance floor where Pierre waited.

"I'll walk you out." He held out his arm.

"Thanks." I took his arm, and he led me to the exit. I made one last glance over my shoulder to see Denise and Estelle dancing and laughing together while Antonia surveyed the throng of drabs for potential danger. "She can't know."

"Pardon?"

"My friend who's currently dancing with Estelle. She's my work supervisor. She can't know about my involvement with Gregor."

Pierre patted my hand. "Estelle will protect your secret. Gregor has sworn us all to secrecy. You are his and he will protect you."

Somehow, that didn't make me feel better.

FIFTEEN

I blinked down at the red-stained floor and swallowed the involuntary response to gag. The placement and sheer volume of the blood suggested at least five victims had died in a circle in the middle of a living room, blood pooling under their bodies and soaking into the trendy area rug. The nearby couch and wall on the one side were covered in blood spatter as were the television and framed family photographs on the other wall.

When I'd arrived, Kang had dismissed the lingering analysts so we had the apartment to ourselves to stare at all the bloody chaos.

"Are you going to be okay?" Kang asked. He stood at my side, his silent presence offering a weird sort of comfort that I'd grown accustomed to without realizing it.

"I'm fine."

"You look green."

"I'll be fine," I amended.

He leaned in, his hand trailed up my arm and he whispered in my ear, "You're such a liar."

I swatted his hand away and swayed on my feet. "Stop distracting me. What exactly am I looking at? And where's Jacobs?"

"You're looking at evidence suggesting five bodies had been arranged in a circle, and Jacobs is still finishing up at Odette's apartment."

"Lucky bastard."

"I'll tell him you said so."

"You're just trying to sabotage our relationship." I lifted my chin.

"Of course. I want you all to myself."

I walked around the blood-stained floor. "Not sure why you called me in. Not that I mind billing the department for the call fee, but there are no bones here."

"Ah, well. That wouldn't be entirely accurate." Kang remained where I'd stood earlier, tracking my progress with his gaze. "Take a look at the coffee table."

I turned and walked over to the coffee table someone had pushed to the side of the room. An evidence bag sat on the scratched laminate covered surface.

"Is that...?"

"A severed finger? Yes. We were hoping to find

more—at least some bone fragments, but this crime scene is clean. A finger is enough, right?"

"It is." I snatched the evidence bag from the table and walked back over to the pools of blood. "Clean wouldn't be the word I'd use to describe this scene."

Kang shrugged. "Aside from the blood, severed finger and summoning circle, there's no evidence. No signs of struggle, no chunks of hair or skin. No bloody footprints. It's incredibly odd."

I knelt near the stained area rug. Specs of white powder speckled the floor not soaked with blood. "A summoning circle?"

"It appears so. Preliminary results indicate it's made of regular table salt."

"So they summoned something and it killed them before arranging them in a neat little circle? Or someone else used their deaths to summon something inside the circle? Or..."

"We have an occult specialist as a consultant as well. We might have to call them in. But in the meantime, I was hoping you could get something from the finger. Only if you're up to it, though." His gaze softened and dropped to scan my body as if looking for visible signs of an impending breakdown.

I narrowed my eyes. "Did you call me in just to check up on me?"

"Maybe." He clamped his mouth shut.

"You could've just called and asked me if I was okay."

"And you would give an honest answer? Or would you tell me everything was fine?"

I opened and closed my mouth. He knew me well. That was exactly what I would've told him, but only because it was the truth.

"I needed to see you for myself," he said, like he was admitting something terrible. "You had a gun pressed to your head. That's not a normal everyday thing to get over and if the severity of the incident hasn't hit you yet, it will later. Hell, I don't think I've recuperated from witnessing it. I'm using every ounce of self-control not to storm into the precinct, find the guy, and..." He pressed his lips together.

"You tackled him to the ground and I tortured him with a spirit."

His gaze flashed. "It wasn't enough."

I didn't have the guts to ask him what would be enough, so instead, I said, "I really am fine."

"You should see a therapist."

"I've been talking to one since I met you," I lied. I had no problem with seeing a therapist, it was more a matter of time and money, both of which I had little of. I waved at the pools of blood. "Do you have any names?"

"We didn't find any identification, but the apartment is registered to Timothy Richards."

"I hope you brought some chickens."

"You get three." He pointed at the hallway.

"That's rather ambitious." I only had one finger to work with.

"We were hopeful we'd find more bones. Maybe even some skull fragments." He leaned in, his words a caress along my skin. "And I know you can do more than you let on."

As if listening to our conversation, the chickens clucked at each other, followed by a flutter of wings.

Instead of confirming Kang's suspicions, I sighed and retrieved a chicken. She was flapping around inside the bathtub of the main washroom and had pretty brown feathers. As soon as I picked her up, she nestled into the heat of my body. I held her close and walked back to the living room to join Kang. "If I ever raise more than two bodies for you, it has to be left out of your reports."

Kang raised his eyebrows.

"Even raising two sets me apart," I explained.

Kang shook his head.

"It's not good for me to stand out as a glamy." I didn't really want to explain why. Gregor had found me because of my skill level. Power drew other power. Those who had lots of it wanted to amass even more by either pulling in other strong glamies, or by eliminating them. Either way, being known as a powerful necromancer placed me in more danger especially when I had serious deficits in my training and foundational knowledge. The one person who could train me had disappeared from my life fifteen years ago.

I shouldn't have to explain any of this to a glamy who pretended to be a drab.

"That's not why I shook my head," Kang said.

I waited.

"You already stand out, Lark," he said, his expression growing serious. "With or without your magic."

"Sure."

"You do," he said, voice firm. "To me."

The tension in my shoulders faded and I stood still, holding a chicken and met Kang's smouldering gaze. "You need to stop saying sweet things."

"Why's that?"

"I'm about to sacrifice a chicken and it's going to kill the mood."

"I'm pretty sure you could be drenched in blood spatter, and I'd still want you, but I'll play by your rules." He held his hands up and stepped back. "For now."

Not knowing what to say to...that...I turned away from Kang and opened the evidence bag. I withdrew the finger, cold to the touch. The edges were raw and jagged, suggesting the finger had been torn off instead of neatly severed with a weapon. Kang reached out and plucked the evidence bag from my hand. He'd have to record the raising to maintain chain of custody.

With the bloody finger in my knife hand, I sacrificed the chicken, murmured the incantation and pulled my magic around me. I didn't know the name of the dead person, so instead of calling the name, I sent my magic rushing through his amputated finger as a call to the soul instead.

Kang stepped in and relieved me of the chicken's body. He'd bag and seal it for me while I spoke to the spirit.

A spectre materialized above the pools of blood, floating at eye level. The man had one of those faces that still had a youthful roundness to the cheeks even though the lines on his forehead and neck clearly indicated he'd seen some decades.

"My name is Lark Morgan," I said. "I'm sorry to call you from your resting place. I'm a necromancer on contract with the Victoria Police Department and we'd like to know who or what did this to you and your companions."

The spirit continued to hover over one of the pools of blood, bobbing in the air like a floatation device in the ocean.

Nothing.

"I'm sorry we don't know your name yet. Can you tell me?" I asked.

The spirit continued to lock his unblinking gaze on me but didn't reply.

"Can you bring me another chicken?" I asked Kang.

Normally, I didn't have to put much effort into calling spirits or getting them to answer my questions. Only glamies presented any kind of resistance, and even the few I'd raised in the past had been no match for my power.

Kang grunted and walked away, presumably to get another chicken, but I kept my focus on the non-compliant spirit. Drawing from the well of power inside me, I pulled more magic and wrapped it around the soul. "Answer me."

The spirit jerked and writhed but didn't speak.

Kang nudged my arm and handed over another chicken. Without turning, I gently took the hen from his hands. I didn't waste time. Using my knife, I ended another life to gain power over the dead.

With the new sacrifice, my magical pull on the spirit strengthened. I clutched his severed finger and let the sacrificial blood and my power soak in. Then I squeezed, pushing more and more power into the finger to reach the bone.

I poured my command into my voice. "*Tell me your name.*"

As if someone grasped him by the waist and violently shook him, the spirit thrashed back and forth. His mouth dropped open to emit a high-pitched scream.

"YOUR NAME."

More screaming.

"Who did this to you?"

He convulsed.

"Tell me what happened."

His spirit form wavered and separated before coming back together again.

"Lark," Kang's deep voice interrupted me. "Lark, let him go."

I jerked back and ripped my gaze away from the screeching soul. Kang had taken the second chicken from me at some point and bagged it, and now he held my arm and studied me with concern. His eyes were dark pools I could easily drown in.

"You're destroying his soul. Let him go."

I turned back to the spirit. Kang was right. Something prevented the spirit from answering me. Like a vicious game of tug-a-war, something, or someone, pulled on the spirit from their end with enough power to combat mine. And the poor man's soul was caught in the middle.

I whispered the incantation to release the spirit. He faded away instantly.

My stomach sunk and nausea rolled around my gut, threatening to rush up. I'd tormented a spirit and hadn't realized it as soon as I should have. Would I have stopped if Kang hadn't warned me? I took a long, shaky breath in and focused on the floor in front of me.

"Too bad we don't have the bodies," I said. "We could check to see if their tongues were removed." Though the police had identified the remains of Amelia and Amy, the bodies were too decomposed to discover the missing tongues from their remains alone. We'd only figured out this detail because I'd called their spirits and noticed they had no tongues. If we had the bodies of the victims from this scene, they would've been fresh, and it would've taken seconds to check whether they had their tongues or not.

"Those cases are probably not linked to this one," Kang said, dashing my hopes with a single sentence. "The victims here died a horrific death and left no trace of their bodies. Amy and Amelia were both women who were shot and had their bodies dumped in remote locations. The manner of death alone suggests different killer profiles."

I plucked the evidence bag from his hand and dropped the severed finger inside before releasing it. "I know. It's just that I've gone my whole career never having issues getting a spirit to talk, and now all of a sudden, it feels like every case."

Kang stepped closer and brushed the hair from my face, gently tucking it behind my ear. "The cases aren't linked, but it does seem odd that we have two separate sets of murders with a similar issue. You're not at fault, though, Morgan. This isn't on you. They required five people and a summoning circle to rouse whatever it is they called, and they all died for it. Maybe it's for the best that you didn't win that battle. I'd hate to see what could've been pulled over to our side."

I shivered.

Kang remained close, his hand still near the side of my face. His gaze dropped to my mouth and his thumb stroked my chin. "Let me take you home."

A different kind of shiver shimmied along my limbs. As much as I loved the sound of that, I had unfinished business. Death magic still clung to my skin, unused and unanswered, and I knew just what to do with it.

"I have some client business to finish up."

"I could wait for you and drive you home after."

God, that was tempting, but if I went into an enclosed private space with this man right now, the angry magic pulsing in my veins might try to find another form of release and I wanted to start things right with Kang.

Maybe.

Or I could just take him home now and skip all that dating stuff.

I bit my lip. "No, thank you. I need you to have something to look forward to tomorrow."

Kang grumbled and dropped his hand. "I've given you a lift home before."

"Yeah, but now it's..." My brain fumbled to find the right words.

He raised his eyebrows.

"Different."

His gaze darkened with all kinds of salacious promises and all the air in my lungs escaped my body. He leaned in, close enough to kiss and growled, "I want to see you out of all that leather, Morgan."

I sucked in a breath. Heat spread through my body.

"So dress casually for our date."

CHAPTER
SIXTEEN

With my flashlight in one hand and the spare chicken from the summoning circle slaughter in the other, I stomped through the cemetery while I replayed Kang's words.

Dress casually? Did he plan for us to spend our date watching television or gaming from the couch, or did he want me to dress casually because it was easier to rip off the clothes?

God, why did both those answers sound so appealing right now?

I shook my head and focused on the tombstones and markers as I walked past. The undertaker hadn't returned my calls, but I didn't want to wait any longer to raise Lily's soul and help her find peace. With every-thing else going on, I needed to close this case and even though the adrenaline from raising the crime scene victim and seeing Kang still raged in my blood, I didn't want to put this off any longer.

Besides, I had a date tomorrow night. The promise in Kang's heated gaze was enough to keep me warm all night.

And I'd enjoy my time more, knowing I had one less thing on my plate to deal with professionally.

I might not understand why Cathy was willing to foot the bill for this, but I also wasn't a total asshole. I'd find Lily regardless and send her to the veil. She deserved to rest.

Following the markings, I found my way to Lily Zheng's grave.

And froze.

The turned-up dirt stared back in silent protest.

I walked around the gravesite and cursed. Someone had dug up Lily's grave. She might not be a ghost after all. She might be at the beck and call of a necromancer.

Another necromancer?

Or the same one who raised Candace MacKinnon's murder-loving ghost from our last case? Was there a vigilante death raiser running around the Greater Victoria area trying to exact revenge and cause magical mayhem?

Or was this something else? When did Lily's bones go missing? Before or after I told Cathy the exact location of her grave?

No matter.

I only needed one bone to rip her away from someone else's control.

I toed the dirt. It was dry, but that didn't tell me much. With the summer heat during the day and early evening, this could be a more recent dig.

I hopped down into the open grave and flipped back the lid of the coffin.

And cursed again.

Empty.

Completely fucking empty.

I had to be the biggest fucking failure. I couldn't get victims from multiple crime scenes to talk and now this.

With a snarl, I set the chicken down and patted the interior of the satin-lined box, but nothing remained of Lily Zheng. This coffin wasn't just empty, it had been cleaned, the contents vacuumed out.

I groaned and moved the chicken to the ground outside the grave so I could pull myself out. The chicken clucked and pecked at the dirt around my feet as I slid my phone from my pocket and dialled Cathy.

"Hello?" Cathy answered the phone exactly the same way she always did—like she was a little stunned someone had called her. With caller ID, she had to know I was on the other end, yet her nervous, wavering tone implied she wasn't quite certain who had called.

"Hi, Cathy. It's Lark Morgan from Raisers."

"Oh, hi. How are you?"

I sighed and brushed the dirt from my leather pants. "I'm fine, but we have a problem."

Silence.

"Someone dug up Lily Zheng's grave," I said while unease prickled my skin. I had told Cathy where to locate Lily's remains, and now they were gone. This couldn't be a simple coincidence, could it?

"Do you know anything about this?" I asked.

"What?" Cathy asked.

"Did you dig up Lily Zheng's grave?" I clarified.

"Why would I dig up her grave? Isn't that..." She dropped her voice. "Isn't that what I'm paying you to do?"

"It is, but I still needed to ask."

More silence, and then, "Well...can't you still do your thing? Use her bones and lay her to rest?"

"They took all the bones," I said.

"Why..." Cathy took a deep breath. "Why would someone do that?"

"I'm not sure. It's either to do the same thing we planned to do or a more nefarious reason."

"Like what?" she asked.

"Like controlling her spirit to do their bidding," I answered.

"That's not good."

"No, it often doesn't end well." I took another deep breath. The hen flapped her wings and strutted past me to another section of grass.

"What do we do now?" Cathy asked.

"I feel it's best for you to let this one go."

She hesitated. "Just like that?"

"Look, you can find a new apartment, spend even more money and try to get a witch to ward your current apartment, or you can continue to coexist with Lily's presence outside your apartment once a month."

Cathy sighed. "There's nothing more you can do?"

"I can try to track down who took the bones," I said. "But it will cost you, I'm not a private investigator, and it might be a fruitless search."

Cathy took a moment before responding. Maybe she needed the time to think, maybe she needed the time to choose her words carefully. Whatever the case, her next words came out slow. "Thank you for your effort. I think I will take your advice and let this go."

I nodded, though Cathy couldn't see me. She sounded sincere in her surprise and concern, but something about this whole case still set me on edge. I was missing something. "I think that's for the best."

After we said goodbye and hung up, I called the police station and reported the grave theft. The next of kin would be notified and maybe, just maybe, the bones would be located one day, and Lily could finally get the rest she deserved.

SEVENTEEN

Wearing nice jeans and a simple T-shirt, I stood outside a dog shelter holding the leash to a seventy-pound Samoyed-mix named Buddy and questioned my life choices. So far, the dog hadn't barked at me, nor had he tried to snap off my hand.

Kang looked up from petting the red-nosed pit bull who was currently trying to clean Kang's entire face with his tongue. The off-mode detective wore dark denim jeans that hugged his butt and thighs and gave me all sorts of ideas of what to grab other than this leash, while his graphic shirt showed off his wide shoulders and powerful arms and did things to my heartrate. He had no business being that devastating to look at. Somehow, he managed to become more delicious now than he had solving crimes. I never thought he'd top that.

Kang had already told me to dress casually, so at least I'd guessed my outfit right. Guessing the activity? Not so much.

"Not what you had in mind?" Kang asked.

"Er...just...unexpected." Which was kind of a lie because I didn't know what to expect for a date with grumpy-pants Kang. I'd expected the unexpected and while I wouldn't have been surprised by whips and chains, a wholesome evening dog walking shocked me.

Not sure if it said more about me or my perception of Kang.

He hesitated. "We can skip this part and go straight to dinner if you prefer?"

The Samoyed looked up at me and panted.

"It's not that. I just don't have a good track record with dogs." Why weren't they growling at me yet?

"You mentioned not wanting a dog before. More than once, actually." A smile tugged at his lips. "Didn't peg you for a cat person."

"I have Maggie." Why did I sound so defensive? "And what's wrong with cat people? They're awesome."

"Nothing's wrong with cat people. I've just always pictured you with something more unusual, like a goat with attachment issues or a four-eyed snake named Hector." Kang said. "And Maggie is different."

"I love goats." I ruffled the Samoyed's head.

"I know."

I loved Maggie even more. Kang knew my cat's

story—he'd been one of the detectives on the case—Bernie's case. I'd taken Maggie home after my part in the investigation ended, but I would've taken Maggie home if she'd been a turtle with three legs or a parrot with a swearing problem. She just happened to be a cat.

Kang straightened and the pitty whined. The dog butted his block head under Kang's hand, a silent demand for more attention.

"You love animals, Lark," Kang said. "What's the issue with dogs and why have you looked so sad every time you mentioned them in the past?"

"Dogs don't like me, okay?" I said. "I always assumed it had something to do with the death magic." Even though my death magic seemed to calm all other animals in my proximity.

Looking completely unfazed, Kang nodded at the Samoyed. "Seems like Buddy likes you plenty."

"These are the first two dogs that haven't growled at me on sight." I narrowed my eyes. Normally, dogs appeared ready to rip my head off, but these two looked besotted. "Did you resort to drugging them before I arrived?"

Kang laughed. His smile transformed his face from the detached beauty I always associated with him into something else...something more.

"I didn't drug them, but I do have a way with dogs." He paused and glanced down the street. "So I assume based on your history, you haven't done a lot of dog walking?"

"That's putting it mildly, but yeah." And now, with Kang's presence somehow masking my death energy, I'd have a chance to see what all the fuss was about.

My eyes stung. I thought I'd hidden how much dogs reacting to me so negatively pained me. Yet, Kang had somehow sensed how much I wanted a connection with dogs and made it happen.

Kang.

Don't you dare cry.

"Shall we?" Kang waved at the sidewalk.

"Yeah." I sniffed and looked away. Kang might like me, but he might also think twice about dating me if I started crying on our first date because I got to play with dogs for the first time.

"Let's go along Waterfront Trail," he said. "Unless there's somewhere else you'd like to go?"

"No...no, this is great." I swallowed my emotions and managed to make eye contact with Kang. "Thank you."

His gaze softened. He hadn't missed a damn thing. "This way."

We walked away from the shelter and made our way to Holland Point Park, entering off Dallas Road. The trails lining the rocky beach provided beautiful views of the Salish Sea and the mountain ranges across the channel. Usually, the wind whipped by this southern region of Vancouver Island, leaving everyone cold even on a summer's day, but today was an exception. The wind had decided to stay calm for my date with Kang.

"Is this what you do in your spare time? The grisly detective secretly has a soft side, but can only express himself through his love for animals?"

Kang narrowed his eyes.

I paused and lifted my ear to the sky as if trying to listen for something.

Kang's frown deepened.

"Do you hear that?" I asked.

"All I hear is you speaking nonsense, Lark."

"It's Hallmark calling. They have a corporate businesswoman who's forgotten the true meaning of Christmas and they need you to melt her heart."

Kang shook his head. He stopped walking to stare at me.

I stopped and stared back. I could get lost in his dark brown gaze and that both delighted and scared me at the same time.

"Well, that's a problem," he said.

"Why?"

"I don't want to melt the fictitious heart of some theoretical business woman," he said. "I only want to melt yours."

Heat spread through my body and an invisible band tightened around my chest. He didn't need to do any sort of thing; it had already been melted by that single line. "My heart isn't frozen, Kang."

Hell, if I let my knees buckle, I'd melt into a puddle right now.

Instead, I started walking again, not quite sure how to deal with the intensity surrounding us.

Without a word, Kang walked along beside me, a small smile tugging at the corners of his lips.

"Your heart might not be frozen..." Kang stepped behind me to let a mom jogging behind a double stroller pass. "But maybe you could stop calling me by my last name on our date?"

The Samoyed barked in agreement.

Traitor.

I ignored Buddy and widened my eyes theatrically. "I wasn't aware you had a first name."

He moved back to walk beside me again. "It's Connor and yes, you damn well know it, you little minx." He looked ready to pin me against a tree to teach me a lesson. And now I wanted to defy him just to see what would happen.

"Okay, Connor. Calm down."

Amusement danced in his gaze. Or maybe it was something else. Maybe he just liked hearing me say his name.

"Connor," I repeated, dropping my voice a little lower. "Connor, Connor, Connor..."

He smiled and looked away, a rosy tint colouring his normally pale cheeks.

"So...besides wanting me to say your name. Is there anything else in particular you'd like to talk about?" I asked. "I kind of feel like we're already past the first date get-to-know-you questions."

In fact, the moment Connor asked me out, it felt like we were already in a relationship, despite this being our first date. When Connor said this wouldn't be casual for him, he wasn't joking.

"I know I should probably answer with something witty about exactly how I'd like you to say my name," Connor said. "But I really want to know why you went to Spiral after I warned you away from it."

I narrowed my eyes. How the heck did he know I hit the club last night? Did he have me under surveillance or the club?

I mentally face-palmed.

Argh!

Of course, the VicPD would have Spiral under surveillance, and of course, they would make note of Estelle arriving and who she arrived with. I wasn't being watched, but I'd definitely been caught.

I groaned and squeezed my eyes shut.

Buddy chose that moment to find something particularly interesting off the sidewalk and lurched in that direction, yanking me with him. I staggered to the side and cursed as he led me through tall, wheat-coloured grass.

Buddy wagged his bushy white tail and snuffled the underside of a dense green bush.

"This better not be a dead body," I said. It wasn't. I'd sense the death energy, but I'd once told Ka... Connor...that I'd never get a dog or take up running for fear of discovering bodies. It definitely seemed like a thing.

"No, just a partially eaten hot dog," Connor said.

I peered over to the side, trying to see past the fluff and failed. "How do you know?"

He shrugged and looked away. "I thought I saw the wrapper. You know, those white ones with the ruffled edges."

I sighed and tugged on the leash, not hard, just a gentle tug to say, "Let's go."

Buddy immediately popped his head up and panted over his shoulder at me.

"He's having the time of his life," I said.

"And he saved you from answering my question."

"Saved me? He saved you. I was about to ask why you were following me." My words might've been snappy, but I already knew the answer.

"The place was under surveillance. But also, Jacobs was there. He was following up with questions about the security feed for our last case, and discreetly trying to observe the owner."

"I thought you already served a warrant and grabbed the files." And everyone in the precinct had watched the footage of us dirty dancing. Heat flamed my cheeks.

Connor grimaced. His gaze cut away while he

probably deliberated whether to tell me about the dancing. "About that security footage..."

"Jacobs already told me."

He swallowed and nodded. "I'm sorry. I would've preferred to keep that moment just between us."

"It is between us. Your colleagues are a bunch of perverts."

He laughed and shook his head. "I'm still debating how to sneak the files out of the evidence room without jeopardizing the case."

"Why would you do that? So no one else can watch us or because you want the footage all to yourself?"

Something flashed in his gaze, something dark and seductive and it pulled me in. I wanted to see more of this side of Connor, more of this simmering heat. "Maybe it's a little bit of both."

With a small step, he moved in close, his body brushing mine, his head angled down to peer into my eyes.

I sucked in a breath. Close up, Connor did things to my heart.

"And maybe..." He licked his lips. "Maybe I decided that I'd prefer to make newer, hotter memories with you rather than trying to relive an old one."

We were in the middle of a park. Now was not the time or place to jump Connor. I squeezed my eyes shut and took a deep breath.

"You smell delicious, Lark," he whispered.

"Let's get back to the warrants before my mind goes completely into the gutter."

"Why? Mine's already there and would enjoy the company."

I groaned and opened my eyes to find Connor's gaze flashing with amusement and irresistible heat. "Why? Because we're in public."

"Fine." He stepped away and took his warmth with him. I immediately wanted him back.

"We'll continue this part of the conversation later," Connor continued. "Getting back to Spiral...we got the footage, but we wanted to go farther back to see if we could identify the necromancer responsible. But that's not the point. The point is while Jacobs was there, he saw you dancing with Estelle on the security feed."

Unlike Connor, I couldn't compartmentalize and switch gears as well nor as quickly. My body still thrummed with need, and I swallowed, trying to ignore the heat pooling low in my belly. I went over what Connor said about Jacobs spotting me on the security feed and it helped like a bucket of ice water over the head.

"Wow," I finally managed. "Jacobs must have eagle eyes because the place was packed last night."

"Lark..." Connor pressed his lips together.

Gentle wind rolled off the ocean and brushed my hair across my face. I tucked the errant strands behind my ear and kept my attention on Connor. "What aren't you telling me?"

"He spotted you because all the security cameras were trained on you."

A shiver went up my spine and clamped to the back of my neck. Any lingering heat from Connor's earlier teasing fled. "Oh."

"Yeah. *Oh.*"

I sighed. "Look, I wasn't trying to be belligerent or defiant. I agreed with you that going to Spiral was dangerous and ill-advised. I was with Estelle, though. She's a fucking badass and she brought two vampire guards with her. She also had her heart set on going and I couldn't think of a good excuse to refuse without providing details of your open investigation. I figured I'd be safe as long as I stayed close to Estelle."

Connor sighed and leaned down to pet the pitty. The dog looked up at him adoringly, his wide mouth open and his long tongue lolling to the side.

"I get it," he said. "I just don't like that this guy seems infatuated with you."

"Maybe he was watching me because he knows I work with you. This might not be what it seems."

He studied me for a few tense seconds, a flurry of emotions flashing in his gaze before he looked away again. He seemed to do that a lot around me—as if he feared I'd see something he wasn't prepared to share yet.

"Are you planning to march over to the club and threaten Grant like you threatened your coworkers over the dancing video?"

Connor scoffed. "I didn't threaten them."

I raised my eyebrows.

"Okay, maybe a little. Shaw's terrified of me now."

So Jacobs had lied to me. That was why Shaw had given me that strange look earlier. "I think everyone is terrified of you except Jacobs."

"And you," he said. He watched me intently again, as if my response really mattered, even though he should already know the answer. "I don't intimidate you at all."

"Nope," I agreed. "I've never been scared of you."

We continued to walk along the path at a relaxed pace, comfortable silence settling over us. The wind ruffled my hair and the seagulls' loud chatter filled my ears.

"Why don't you have a dog of your own?" I finally asked.

He pondered my question for a few steps, looking down at the pitty. "I don't live a life that lends itself well to having a dog. It's not fair to them."

"So, you go to the shelter and walk these guys." Look at me go. I'd make detective in no time if they actually let me join the force.

"As often as I can," he said.

"You like dogs that much?"

He hesitated before answering. "These animals have a way of taking away all the stress of my job. Maybe it's how they live in the moment. Maybe it's their unconditional affection and trust. I don't know.

But this is how I unwind. This is how I get my mind to reset. It's not just the dogs. It's the whole thing—walking, fresh air, listening to nature..."

"This is your happy place," I finished.

He scrunched up his face. He wasn't the type of person to use that term willingly. "I guess you could say that."

He looked away again, apparently transfixed by a passing boat, but I finally figured out one of his tells.

"And you brought me here." I swallowed. He'd brought me to his happy place.

He finally looked back at me, a war of emotions flickering across his expression. He reached out and held my free hand. "Yes. I brought you because I want you here. I wasn't joking when I said this wouldn't be a casual thing between us. I'm all in, Lark."

"And what if this doesn't work out?" I waved my hand between the two of us. "What if we're not compatible?"

"Like sexually, or..."

"All of it."

"We're compatible," he said firmly.

"You're awfully confident for someone who spends half his time in my presence glaring at me."

He nodded, a slow smile spreading across his face. "I've already made peace with being stuck with you one way or another."

I snorted. The sound was the exact opposite of ladylike. "You're so sweet."

"You don't like me because I'm sweet."

That actually wasn't true. Connor was sweet. He was considerate. He'd saved my life six years ago. He'd searched for my father. He looked out for me at crime scenes.

Kang did a lot of things to help me and those around him, but he did it in such a subtle way to avoid any kind of fanfare. I definitely liked him because of his sweet side. But I adored those rough edges of his as well. "And why do I like you then?"

His smile widened.

"No, tell me. I've been wondering the same thing myself."

He leaned in. "You like me because I present a mystery to that brain of yours and your curiosity can't help itself."

"I'll find out all your secrets, Connor," I pointed out. "What happens then? What happens when you have no mysteries left to keep me hooked?"

"You'll be so enamored with my wit and charm, that won't be an issue."

I laughed softly and shook my head. I was already enamored, and he knew it. "Geez, I'd love to have some of your confidence."

"Only with you." His expression grew serious, his mouth pressed together, his eyebrows furrowed. "I want you in my life. I want you to be a part of my fucking happy place." He paused. "Is that okay?"

It was more than okay. It was perfect. My heart

melted some more, and I squeezed his hand back. "Yeah. That's okay."

It was more than okay.

It was everything.

WE NEVER MADE it to the restaurant. Instead, we'd grabbed food from a street vender and found a bench to watch the setting sun. Neither of us were the wine-and-dine type, though part of me wanted to drag Connor to a club just so we could dance together again.

The dogs flopped down at our feet and panted happily. The full moon was already visible, becoming more pronounced as the sun inched below the horizon.

"How are you feeling?" I finally asked after our conversation faded into another relaxed silence.

Connor glanced over, his pizza halfway in his mouth. Lowering his food so it hovered over the flimsy paper plate, he answered, "I'm fine, but why do I feel like that was a loaded question?"

I peered up at the night sky before asking another question. "Not feeling hostile?"

His frown deepened. "No..."

"Agitated?"

"Not before, but now that you mention it, this line of questioning is—"

"Wolfish?" I bit my lip.

Understanding flashed across Connor's face and he laughed. He dropped his pizza on the paper plate and laughed some more, a deep rumble of laughter that brought a smile to my face even though I was pretty sure he was laughing at me. "Did you seriously choose the night of a full moon for our date to see if I was a werewolf?"

I took a bite of my hotdog. "Mmmm."

"I could've rescheduled," he pointed out.

I chewed my food and grinned at him. "That would've told me what I needed to know."

"I'm not a werewolf, Lark."

"Clearly." I was out of options. He wasn't fae, and he wasn't a werewolf. Those were the two types of glamies I knew of that could smell, see, and hear spirits other than necromancers.

"I could just tell you," he said.

"Don't you dare. I'm having too much fun trying to figure it out. Besides, you don't want to relieve me of my curiosity before I'm properly enamored by your wit and charm."

He rested his plate on his lap and leaned back. The moonlight danced along his chiselled features. "Are you not enamored already?"

"Maybe."

His lips twitched, but he didn't say more.

I wanted to reach out with my fingers and trace those lips, then the hard lines of his nose, cheekbones, and jawline. When I first met him, I'd thought he looked a little like a younger, clean-cut Keanu Reeves. Still did, but somehow the comparison didn't fit as well anymore. Connor was just...Connor. And he was gorgeous.

He peered over at me. "I don't think you're ready to find out, anyway," he said.

"You're probably right."

Buddy whined and rested his fluffy head on my foot. I broke the rest of my hot dog in two and gave both dogs a piece. They inhaled the food and looked at me expectantly. I reached out and scratched behind Buddy's ear. "I know you were caught between protecting your family and wanting to be honest with me, but why...why did you make me feel like you didn't like anything about me?"

"I liked and like plenty."

"You have a funny way of showing it."

The muscles along his jawline bunched as he clenched his teeth. He didn't speak right away. When he did, he lowered his voice, the deep tone rumbling from his chest. "I have to keep a part of me separate when I'm doing my job. I can't allow myself to feel too much. It sometimes comes across as unfriendly."

Sometimes?

Seriously, sometimes?

In other words, Connor compartmentalized. Not sometimes, though. All the time. And unfriendly wouldn't be the word I'd use to describe his demeanour at a crime scene. "I would've said hostile, but there's no point arguing semantics."

"Ah, yes. And you're a ray of sunshine."

"Compared to you, I'm incandescent," I muttered.

His lips twitched and he leaned back on the bench, his pizza forgotten. I had the random thought of picking up the plate and tossing it to the side so I could straddle him on the park bench. His snark did nothing to repel my growing attraction, and if I were being completely honest with myself, this attraction had been building since the moment I met him.

I blinked the fantasy away.

"I wasn't being sarcastic," Connor said.

"Shocking."

His lips quirked up at the corners. "You are like a ray of sunshine when you enter a crime scene. I mean… generally, you look like you just sucked on a lemon, but you still manage to lift the mood."

"Would you prefer I smiled maniacally while I dispose of the chickens?" Sucked on a lemon? How dare he?

"Of course not," he said. "But even with your pissed off expression, you give us all something else to focus on. Instead of thinking about the brutality laid out in front of me, I'm worried about the feelings of a fucking chicken."

"They're sweet birds," I huffed and folded my arms. "Very misunderstood."

"They're deranged remnants of dinosaurs, but

we're not arguing semantics. Besides, it's quite obvious to me and Jacobs that sacrificing the chickens is one of the parts of your job that really bothers you."

"Sacrifices aren't supposed to be easy," I whispered.

"You're nothing like I thought you'd be when my chief first told me I'd be working with a necromancer." He studied me thoughtfully. "At first, I was angry and insulted he thought we needed help from a death raiser, but I'm glad he made the call. You've been instrumental in solving so many cases."

"And you *like* me." I fluttered my eyelashes.

His lips twitched. "That made it easier in some ways, but also harder."

Do not make a joke about making things hard. Do not make a joke. Don't do it.

Connor would react and while every cell in my body ached with anticipation, I wasn't an exhibitionist. He'd been teasing me all night, taking his time to build a fire. He'd let his gaze and touch linger, he dropped suggestive comments and innuendos. If he touched me now, I'd probably combust and take out the entire block. I didn't trust either of us to wait for privacy to put out the fire.

I cleared my throat and mentally searched for a safer comment or question. "So why didn't you ask me out sooner?"

"Oh, that's easy." He shrugged. "I thought you hated me."

And at times, I did, but not for the reasons he thought. "What gave me away?"

His smile widened. "Our dance."

My skin heated as the memories of that dance surged up. Yes. That dance. I'd like to say that it was all Connor, and the dancing skills definitely were all his, but our dance had been more than great technique with a partner, our dance had been all chemistry.

And we had a lot of it.

The thing with mixing chemicals, though, was we could either create something truly magical or get burned.

Only time would tell.

I WALKED up the front steps to my apartment building acutely aware Detective Connor Kang followed. He placed his hand on my lower back and heat spread through my body as first date jitters tied my stomach into a giant knot. I dug my keys out of my purse, thankfully finding them on the first attempt. That didn't say much, I hadn't brought my regular monstrosity.

I didn't want tonight to end. As far as I was concerned, this had been the perfect date.

The sunset had been beautiful, and our conversation was open and honest.

We'd returned the dogs to the shelter. Apparently, Connor had a key and a standing agreement he could come and go, day or night, to spend time with the dogs.

When I'd questioned him on it, he'd merely shrugged and told me it was cheaper than therapy.

Connor stepped closer and leaned down, his hand cupped my face, and his gaze swept over my body.

He was going to kiss me. And I would love it. Every second of it, and then I'd invite him up to my apartment and do very, very naughty things to him and with him.

I licked my lips.

Something vibrated.

Connor flinched before refocusing on my face.

His phone vibrated again. He swore and stepped back. "I'm on call."

"It's okay." And it was. We both had taxing jobs that had a way of interfering with our lives.

Connor looked like he wanted to say more but answered the call instead. "Kang, here."

"Connor..." Jacobs spoke loud enough for me to catch snippets. "Need...help...on..."

Connor checked his watch and cursed again. "I'll be there in ten minutes."

And there went my plans for the rest of the evening. My heart sunk and the butterflies that had been fluttering in my belly collapsed. But, if Jacobs needed help, he needed help. "Can I do anything?"

"Not with this one." He leaned down and pressed

a tender kiss on my cheek. "We'll talk soon. You have your keys?"

I held them up and shook them. The metal jangled.

He nodded and hesitated to study my face one last time, his expression torn.

"Go," I said. "Jacobs needs you and I'm not going anywhere. We can pick this up another night."

"Be careful what you promise." He winked and squeezed my hand before turning away to jog down the stairs.

I didn't know which view I preferred—Connor coming or going.

I paused to smile at the empty street while I stood at my apartment's front entrance.

One thing was for sure, the man certainly knew how to fill a pair of pants.

I unlocked the main door and made my way to my apartment. When I entered, I called out, "Logan? Brandon?"

Neither of them answered. I turned to hang my purse up on its designated hook and saw a sticky note.

It read: *Went out. Don't wait up.*

Typical. Those two were probably out partying hard. We had very different ways of coping with the stress of our jobs. I didn't judge. The boys would come home at a god-forsaken hour, probably with the sun rising shortly after. Then they'd rinse and repeat. I didn't know how either of them did it. I simply didn't have the energy.

Maggie hissed and ran past me to my bedroom. I paused in the living room. Some of the furniture was out of place. That in itself wasn't odd, but an unfamiliar cologne clung to the air.

I sniffed again, but either I imagined things or I'd already acclimatized to the new scent. Unease swirled in my stomach. Even with the cologne smell gone, something was off. Something was wrong. The energies in the room were in turmoil.

Bernie's ghost appeared out of nowhere and pulsed in front of me. *"Run."*

I reached into my pocket to pull out my phone.

A hand clamped over my face, holding a cloth over my mouth and nose. Another arm wrapped around my body, pinning my arms to my sides and preventing me from moving. I thrashed, flailing my legs. The heels of my feet connected with my assailant's shins, and he grunted. His grip loosened. Pushing away, I staggered forward, my brain fuzzy, my limbs heavy, fighting whatever drugs I'd inhaled.

I gasped for air.

The man reached for me, his hand snagged my hair and necklace. Something snapped and metal clattered to the floor.

Fight.

I scrambled, trying to get away, trying to clear the drugs from my lungs with each rasping breath of air. The man used his hold on my hair to push me forward, my legs buckled. I lurched and fell. My body too numb and my brain too scrambled to react, I hit the floor with a loud smack. The man was on me, the cloth over my nose and mouth again. My field of vision narrowed. The edges grew fuzzy and faded. My arms twitched as I tried desperately to move them and use some of my self-defence training.

I should have kissed Connor.

Everything went black.

EIGHTEEN

Hard jostling woke me up. My body slammed into metal. I blinked, but the images around me remained fuzzy and dark. The sharp smell of dirt and rubber burned my nose along with the odour of gasoline.

I was in the back of a truck with a windowless canopy.

Rope chafed the sore skin around my wrists behind my back. My ankles were also tied together, making it difficult for me to brace in any way with each bump and jostle of the truck.

An engine roared.

Weak light streamed through the cracks between the canopy and the tailgate, so it was either early morning or early evening.

Kang's face flashed in my mind. Would he know I had been taken? We didn't have any definitive future plans and I'd already completed the raisings for his current case. Would he text or call after he helped Jacobs and figure out why I didn't respond? Or would he assume my silence was because he'd left our date prematurely?

When would Logan realize I was missing? Would he stumble into the apartment with Brandon and wonder where I was? Or would he assume I left for work? I didn't have regular hours and the nature of both our jobs meant we didn't check in with each other unless a significant portion of time had passed.

When would anyone notice I was gone? Would they see my purse and make the connection in time? What about my phone? I didn't feel it in my pocket, so either my attacker destroyed it, got rid of it, or left it at the apartment.

Or would it be too late when they finally figured it out?

A bump in the road lifted me off the bottom of the truck bed, only to slam me back down. The bed had one of those liners with a beveled surface, so each time I got thrown around, the hard peaks of each ridge jabbed into my body with bruising force. My head spun. My ass and thighs hurt. But aside from a small cut on my forehead, I wasn't bleeding. At least, I didn't think I was.

And that was the unfortunate part. If I had blood, I could possibly do something. Blood and bones.

And I didn't have either. Normally, I'd hesitate to

use my own blood as a sacrifice, but I'd make an exception and risk the veil as an alternative to whatever the fuck this was. Even if I used my own blood, though, I couldn't use my own bones—those had to come from the dead. So without blood and bones, I may as well be a regular human.

Vulnerable. Trapped.

I shivered and tried to peer through the cracks.

Nothing but weak light that seemed to brighten.

Early morning, then.

I must've been out for at least a night. Or even longer. I didn't know a lot about chloroform, but that must've been what the person used on me. Surely, it shouldn't have knocked me out for that long. I must've been drugged with something else afterward.

And who the fuck was responsible for this? Grant? Did his obsession lead him to abduction? Was it the rose giver? Were they one and the same? I had so many questions and no answers. One thing was certain, this person was taking me for a little field trip, and I needed my energy for whatever he had planned.

It had to be Grant—that creepy motherfucker. I should've kneed him in the balls in addition to stomping on his feet when I'd had the chance.

I curled up on my side to better brace myself against the sides of the truck bed and to prevent myself from getting chucked around with every pothole. Trying to force my breathing into a more regular rhythm, I made my lungs hold air for a couple of seconds longer with each breath.

There. Finally.

Breathing established.

My heartbeat still thudded in my ears and rattled my already-aching brain, and my stomach twisted into a knot, but I had to start somewhere.

With another deep breath, I attempted to reach for my bond with Gregor.

Nothing.

I tried again.

A faint presence in my blood responded but slipped away when I tried to grab it. My bond with Gregor had run its course. I should've renewed it right away. I should've insisted on raising a third vampire to clear our debt.

The truck kept ambling down the mystery road to my unknown future, leaving me alone with my thoughts.

I didn't like that one bit.

Metal hinges whined as someone opened the upper door of the canopy. I blinked against the harsh daylight streaming into my makeshift prison.

A silhouette stood on the other side of the opening, the bright light blotting out his face.

I blinked again and squinted. Lean and wiry, standing around six feet tall, a man peered into the back of the truck. My vision adjusted and focused on the familiar person standing in front of me. He wore a simple long-sleeved shirt, his chest tattoo peeking out of the top of the neckline. He'd tucked his gold chain under his shirt, but the visible part around his neck glinted in the morning daylight.

"The barista?" What the fuck was his name again? "Steve?"

He smiled and leaned in. "I'm thrilled you remember me."

"I'm not." I tried to peer out of the truck bed, but all I could see was Steve's fake customer service smile and the tops of trees.

"Help," I screeched.

"Go ahead." Steve's smile widened. "Scream some more. I like how it sounds and no one else is around to hear you."

I shut my mouth and glared. "What's your whole plan with this? Are you going to kill me and leave me here?"

He straightened and looked up to consider the sky for a moment. He had an old scar under his chin, most likely from a childhood accident. Logan had something similar after he tried to sled down the stairs and ended up having an unfortunate run-in with the small table at the landing.

"Kill you, yes," Steve answered. "But not right away. As for leaving your remains here? No. Not this time. I think I will leave your broken body on the doorstep of that cop boyfriend of yours. Or maybe after I've cut out your tongue, I'll dismember you and send him little pieces to watch his sanity crumble, piece by fucking piece. He was so smug in my coffee shop. So condescending. I want to rip that confidence from him until he's a shell of a man."

Cut out my tongue?

A cold chill ran along my skin. Cutting out my

tongue like the female victims in the VicPD cases. This wasn't a coincidence.

"You're a fucked-up individual."

"Oh." He finally looked back at me. "You have no idea."

"Why are you doing this?"

"You'll find out soon enough." He jerked his head at me and the truck. "Sit back. I wouldn't want to hurt you prematurely."

"You are the one who sent the flowers, aren't you?"

Steve looked up with a frown. "What flowers?"

"Fuck off, you've already kidnapped me and plan to kill me. What's the harm in fessing up to sneaking into my home and leaving me a rose?"

"Last night was the first time I've set foot in your apartment. I've never left you flowers, though I can leave some on your grave later, if you'd like. It's the least I can do."

Harsh reality slapped me in the face as Steve reached forward and dropped the tailgate of the truck. He pulled out a pocket knife from his tapered black jogging pants.

My brain stuttered while my mouth worked, opening and closing with a mind of its own. I should probably say something. I should beg for my life or demand answers, but instead I sat there awkwardly as Steve leaned into the truck with his knife. Without a word, he reached forward, flicked out the blade, and cut through the rope tying my ankles together. The severed ropes fell away.

As Steve straightened to put away the knife, I scrambled to get my feet under me. With a shrill scream, I jumped out of the truck and barrelled into Steve. I sent him sprawling backward. With no free hands to break my fall, I slammed into him. "Oomph."

I drove my knee up into his groin, rolled off him and staggered to my feet. My core already screamed from overuse.

Not knowing which way to go, I picked a direction and ran.

I didn't get far.

Hands closed around the rope tying my wrists together and pulled me back.

I fell to the ground, ass first, and pain shot up my tailbone.

Steve walked around to stand in front of me. "You're going to regret that." His cold tone certainly sent chills over my skin.

He reached down and hauled me to my feet by my upper arm. His fingers dug into my skin with bruising pressure. With one hand holding my arm, he drew back the other and slammed his fist into my face. Pain shot through my head. I reeled to the side. My head swam and an instant headache bloomed behind my eyes.

"You're not playing by the rules," Steve hissed. "Next time, think about that before trying to defy me."

I straightened and licked my bleeding lip. What was he going to do? Kill me? He already planned to do that. I didn't owe this fucker one single civil word let alone obedience. "Please. I've had dicks slap my face harder than that."

His gaze flashed and he clenched his teeth together, baring them like a wild animal. "You won't be making jokes for long."

"Hardly necessary when you're already the biggest joke here." I clamped my mouth shut. Maybe antagonizing my captor wasn't the best idea, but I couldn't stand here and be nice. I couldn't passively watch some random guy from a coffee shop gut me with a pathetic pocket knife and not insult him.

But I also wanted to escape and not anger him to the point of killing me right away.

Fuck.

I pressed my lips together tighter.

He narrowed his eyes, but instead of hitting me again, he dug his fingers into my arm even harder and hauled me toward the truck.

I could've dragged my feet or tried to kick him. I could've twisted to escape his painful grasp. But what was the point? I wouldn't get far, and he'd probably hit me again. I needed a fully functioning brain to escape this place and despite my bold statement earlier, that punch had hurt.

I pushed my magic out, desperately searching for bones, human bones, but nothing pinged back. If he'd left any bodies in the woods, they were too far away for me to detect. I pulled my magic in and studied my surroundings, flicking my gaze around, trying to gather as much information as possible.

The truck was parked a few feet away, angled in such a way I couldn't see the licence plate number. Not that it mattered. I already knew who the bad guy was. I didn't need to have the cops run his plates.

A small log cabin sat on the other side of the truck. A forest of tall evergreen trees surrounded the entire clearing and spanned endlessly in all directions. It looked like an older forest, with big, well-established trees and little undergrowth. A dirt road led away from the cabin, presumably to the same dirt road we came in on. The air smelled like dry moss, firewood, and pine needles.

Steve had abducted me to the middle of nowhere. How would Kang or Logan find me here?

The answer hit me like a ton of bricks. Air whooshed out of my lungs and left me dizzy.

They wouldn't find me.

No one would.

"We're on an island," Steve spoke in a conversational tone like we gossiped over coffee in his cafe. "I chartered a boat to get here. I like to be alone with my girls. It's a shame you slept through most of the trip."

Girls. Plural. I wasn't the first person he'd brought here. His words confirmed the horrid truth circulating in my mind ever since he mentioned cutting off my tongue.

My stomach twisted.

"There's nothing else on the entire island and the nearest land is at least twenty kilometres away. You'll drown from exhaustion before your feet touch soil again."

Lovely. "You killed those other girls."

"Other girls?"

"We found the remains of two women. Both died of gunshot wounds and the detectives think they're connected. I know the world is fucked up, but the chances of running into two separate killers who like to cut out tongues seems less likely."

He smirked. "Were you helping the police with that? Did you get anything? Learn anything?" He leaned forward, a glint in his gaze. "Were Amelia, Elizabeth and Jessica not super chatty?"

"Elizabeth? Jessica?"

"Oops." He shrugged. "Did I choose wrong? Who did you find?"

I swallowed. "Amy."

"Ah yes...Amy." His smile was slow and gross, and I wanted to punch it off his face. I reached out with my magic again.

Still nothing. No human bones answered my call.

"Why did you go after Odette?" I asked.

He tilted his head. "Odette?"

"Amelia's sister."

He snapped his fingers. "That's right. God, she was so annoying. She kept coming back to the café hoping to retrace her sister's steps because Amelia's last post on social media was a picture of the cappuccino I made her. She used the hashtag blessed." Steve snorted like he found the whole thing funny.

I didn't.

My heart ached for that girl, for that young woman who was enjoying her life and celebrating the little things in life, only to have that beautiful simplicity ripped away from her and have her last moments filled with Steve's company and undoubtedly sheer terror.

"So Odette came to your coffee shop looking for answers and you decided to hire someone to kill her?" Why would a killer hire another killer? "Why not take care of her yourself?"

Steve narrowed his gaze. "I didn't have time to deal with her—not when I had plans for you. I would've just left her alone, but she liked to think of herself as an amateur detective. She still hoped to find her sister and started poking around where she shouldn't. The guy I hired to kill her might've been caught but even if he talked, he doesn't know anything. So if you're hoping that cop boyfriend of yours will somehow figure out where we are and save you, you're going to be disappointed."

"The assassin had Grant's number." A thought slammed into my head, making me wince. "Is he in on this, too?"

"Grant?" Steve smirked. "My business partner is too busy snorting lines of coke and trying to use his position as a club owner to rail young, impressionable women to realize what I've been up to. He doesn't know about this place either."

"Business partner?"

Steve nodded. "I'm a silent partner at Spiral. I don't go there often, but when I saw you in my coffee shop with that cop, and then later make an appearance with those vampires, I couldn't help myself. I snuck into the security room. Almost got busted by a detective, too." Steve licked his lips and smiled. "It was such a rush. Almost as much of a rush as grabbing you. And not a moment too soon, apparently. If I waited too long, your stalker might've beaten me to it."

"My stalker?"

"The person leaving the roses."

"So you know who it is?"

"Not at all, nor do I give a fuck." He reached into the truck and pulled out a rifle. I didn't know much about guns, especially rifles, but it looked like the kind my brother used in his online games to snipe opponents from a distance.

Steve smiled at the rifle and held it up for me to get a better look. "It's a 0.308 Sako 85 Finnlight."

I pursed my lips, hoping my disinterest in his murder weapon of choice would show.

"It won awards because it's reliable and accurate while being lightweight. Bolt action. Mild recoil, proven killing power, and I can hike with it for days. This is a superb hunting rifle."

The memories of the women I'd recently raised flowed through my thoughts. Flashbacks to how they kept trying to run away. Steve had cut out their tongues, but they had been trying to tell me what happened this whole time, and now I was finding out the truth the hard way.

The sick bastard intended to hunt me like a fucking deer.

Ice flowed through my veins and my stomach twisted some more. "Why do you do it?"

He cocked his head.

"Hunt the women. Do you get off on it? Did you not have enough power growing up? Did they reject you? Mommy issues?"

He flinched at the last one.

Bingo.

He didn't hit me again, though. Instead, he slung the rifle over his shoulder using the strap and pulled the knife from his pocket again. Without a word, he roughly spun me around and cut through the rope chafing my wrists. It fell to the ground and my shoulders screamed from the release and instant increase in blood flow.

Before I could stretch or react, his boot connected with the small of my back and pushed, sending me sprawling forward to the ground. My knees hit the dirt first. Pain shot up my legs. I flung my hands out to break my fall. The rocky ground scraped and dug into my palms, slicing the skin open. My head snapped forward, smacking the dirt before rebounding. My mind spun.

"It's time to run," Steve taunted.

I pushed off the ground and stumbled to my feet. My vision wavered. I turned to Steve and found myself looking down the barrel of his favourite hunting rifle.

A memory of having a gun pressed to my temple surged up without warning and froze me on the spot. As if a clamp tightened around my chest, it hurt to breathe. I couldn't move. Another memory of having a gun pointed at me surfaced, one from six years ago that hadn't bothered my thoughts or dreams for a long time. I wheezed in little drags of air.

My heart slammed into my breastbone, over and over again, making it hard to think.

"I'll give you two hours, Lark, and then I'm coming for you." He didn't do any of that Hollywood shit like flick the safety or action the bolt, but looking into the end of the barrel had the same terrifying effect. "Lots of time for you to run and hide. Let's make this a good hunt."

Run and hide? I couldn't even move.

Steve licked his lips. "The time starts now."

Adrenaline kicked in. Fight or flight, and my body chose flight, snapping into motion. I turned and ran. Still bruised from the rough ride in the back of the truck, my legs protested. I wasn't exactly a gym rat.

Though I worked out, I wasn't a marathon runner or professional fighter. I had a brain and raised dead people.

I ran and ran, thinking, "what the fuck" the entire time. My feet hit the uneven ground with loud thuds. My headache grew, my brain knocking against the inside of my skull with each stride.

The physical excursion heated my blood and limbs, but the knowledge that warmed my heart was knowing that regardless of my fate on this island, my brother would eventually find this piece of shit and make him pay.

I might be long gone by then, but Steve's days were numbered, too.

Should I circle back, somehow avoid detection, hide and wait for Steve to set out? What if he spotted me? Would he actually wait two hours? That was a long fucking time, and his word was worth shit. But if I went back and he spotted me, I'd lose any potential lead I currently had.

If I just kept running, though, that wouldn't work either. I had nowhere to run to, I'd fatigue faster, and he'd find me eventually.

I needed to make a trap. Somehow. Or get the truck and drive over Steve.

Oh, I liked that plan.

But first, I needed distance. Distance gave me time and time gave me breathing room to think. Right now, everything burned too much for plotting murder. My lungs burned, my muscles burned, my scraped palms burned, everything fucking burned. And rage spiraled up like a fiery ball of hell.

I had to make sure Steve paid for this with his life.

Or I'd literally die trying.

My feet kept slamming against the uneven path, jarring my body with each stride. The air continued to make my lungs scream in agony as I kept running. Branches snagged my clothes and hair, and the smell of pine, hemlock and cedar flooded my system. It really was just me and Steve on this rock of an island.

Murder Island.

Sweat dripped down my face as I pressed on. If I survived this bullshit, I'd have to thank Kang for telling me to dress casually for our date. I'd already be dead if I had to do this in heels.

No, that wasn't true. I'd ditch the heels, but running barefoot through a forest would still place me at a disadvantage.

Bones. I needed bones.

I pushed my magic out again, scanning for the dead, again and again. And still, nothing. My magic failed to detect anything nearby.

I assessed my surroundings as I continued to run through the trees without any destination. My simple plan was to place as much distance between me and Steve and his nasty rifle that obviously compensated for something.

The land rose to my left and I veered off the path

to cut through the brush. A branch slashed me across the face. Pain spread across my cheek. I clenched my teeth and continued. My lungs were on fire, my legs protested. This pace wasn't sustainable. Hell, prolonged running wasn't sustainable. I might work out to stay in shape, but this wasn't a part of my regular routine.

Bones. Bones. Bones.

I needed bones.

Once again, I sent my magic out, scouring the forest.

Still nothing.

The remains of a few small animals answered my call, but that wasn't enough for a trip to the veil.

I needed bones, blood and power, and right now, I only had two.

The trees thinned out as the sound of waves and seagulls grew louder. I broke from the tree cover and came face to face with a steep incline. An idea formed in my mind despite my raging headache. I paused and tilted my head to listen to the forest around me. Birds tittered their merry songs without any care to my world falling down around me. A gentle breeze moved through the leaves and nearby, ocean waves crashed along the shoreline.

I couldn't hear Steve running or cursing. The sounds consuming my hearing, other than the sounds of nature, were my rasping breath and thundering heart.

I ran around the base of the hill. The cliff dropped off sharply on the other side to overhang the deep ocean. I cautiously stepped to the edge and peered down the sheer drop. No visible rocks jutted out from under the relatively calm water. It looked deep. Real deep.

Perfect.

Should I dive in now and try to swim away?

Or should I stick to my initial plan to pinpoint Steve's location first?

I couldn't keep running, or swimming, I needed to rest and think about options and also, get a better idea of Steve's position. If he lost my trail in the forest, I'd get a longer break and wouldn't need to expose myself to the cold ocean.

Decision made, I scrambled up the side of the cliff. It wasn't easy, nor quick. The rocks dug into my already scratched palms and the jagged edges sliced open my forearms. Sweat poured down my face by the time I made it to the top.

How much time had I wasted climbing this absurd hill? How much had Steve caught up?

Exhausted, I lay on my stomach. The cliff edge with the sheer drop was behind me, the path I'd taken to climb up the hill to my left and the rest of the island, including the gun-toting asshole, in front of me. I had a great view of the forest and would, hopefully, spot Steve if he tracked me this far.

Also, if a boat went by, I had a chance of flagging it,

though I didn't hold a lot of hope for that option. I hadn't spotted any vessels while I climbed this hill and there were no sails dotting the horizon.

Taking in deep breaths, I focused on regaining my strength and controlling my breathing while I continued to wait and think. At least my headache had eased, and my leg muscles ached so much from running and climbing that I no longer felt the bruises from the truck ride.

Small wins.

The plume of smoke in the distance marked the cabin's location and my ultimate goal. I'd wait here until one of two things happened. Either Steve found me and I'd enact Plan B, or someone would magically rescue me.

It was a shit plan, but I had nothing else to work with.

Perched at the top of the cliff, I continued to watch for movement in the forest below.

"Oh, Lark..." Steve's nauseating voice called out from the forest. I pressed my chest to the dirt, my head peeking up between two large rocks at the cliff's edge. My arm wasn't good enough to chuck them and inflict any damage on Steve—a pity—but they provided the cover I needed.

In order for Steve to get to me, he'd have to step out from the trees. He couldn't easily climb this cliff from any of the other directions, so if he spotted me, I'd know.

And then Plan B.

Which was still a ridiculous fucking plan.

"I know I said two hours, Lark, but I couldn't help myself." Steve crooned from somewhere within the protection of the trees.

I swallowed the stomach acid bubbling up my throat.

"I'm very excited to take this to the next level." A branch snapped. I'd tried to cover my tracks, but from the sound of his voice, he headed straight for me.

Almost as if...

Dread clamped my heart. I turned away from the path and patted my body. My necklace was gone, lost in the scuffle at my apartment. I kept searching. Nothing. I emptied my pockets. Nope. I checked my shoes and gasped.

Argh.

Why did I assume anything about this would be fair?

Using my nails, I pried a white pill-sized tracker free from one of the white soles of my running shoes. He must've planted it there when I'd been drugged. I tossed the tracker over the side of the cliff, checked the other shoe and turned back to the path.

Steve stood at the tree line, rifle raised. I dove to the side as a loud bang of a gunshot ripped through the air.

Pain erupted in my arm, and I slammed into the hard-packed dirt of the cliff.

Agony streaked through my body. I cried out and my mind reeled.

Plan B.

Dirt crunched as Steve moved up the path.

Plan B.

"Oh, Larky..."

Plan B.

With pain clamping my mind and my body, I pushed up and rolled. I rolled and rolled and rolled until I rolled right off the cliff into the ocean below.

TWENTY

The cold water closed around me and shocked me out of the pain. My focus narrowed.

Plan B.

My arm was fucked, but the other one still worked and so did my legs.

Positive thoughts only, Lark.

I kicked and pulled, gliding under the water until I couldn't hold my breath any longer. The cool water numbed my skin. My heart slowed down—the beat a deep thud consuming my hearing. My vision narrowed and pressure increased in my head and lungs.

I surfaced, took a deep breath and ducked under again.

It would take Steve at least twenty minutes to make it up that cliff, maybe half that if he was better at climbing than me, which he probably was. By the time he made it to the top and discovered I didn't lay in a puddle of blood, dead, I needed to make it around the point. He'd figure out what I did, but he'd have to climb back down again and then pick a direction. And if luck was on my side, he'd think I died when I fell into the water.

Hopefully, whatever Steve did, I'd have enough of a lead to beat him back to the cabin, find his phone or truck keys, or maybe even another weapon and go from there.

I drew up to the surface again and bobbed in the ocean, sucking in big drags of air. The current had carried me past the cliff and out of view. I took in another deep, ragged breath. I didn't dive under the surface again.

Objective one complete.

Now for the hard part.

I let the current carry me until my toes began to grow numb. Hypothermia set in around twenty to thirty minutes in the coastal waters of British Columbia in the winter, and I didn't have a waiting campfire or dry clothes. Thankfully, it wasn't winter, and the summer weather gave me time to dry and warm up. But the cold water still left my bones numb.

Scrambling up the rocks, I panted and tried to control my breath. My heart raced, beating as though someone punched me from inside my chest with each pump of blood.

How long ago had I hit the water? How much time did I have until Steve caught up?

Had he already reached the top? Would he assume I fell off and died? Or would he assume I was alive?

When I was in the water, I hadn't fought the current—too weak with a wounded arm. If Steve assumed I survived the gunshot, he'd pick this direction because it made the most sense.

Or he'd just go back to the little cabin and wait.

The thought slammed through my brain.

I hadn't thought of that before.

What the hell would I do then? I needed to adjust my plan. Now that I didn't have a tracker in my shoe, Steve would find it a little more difficult to locate me. I needed to put more distance between myself and Steve and find a hiding place.

And then there was the thing I desperately tried to ignore. I couldn't go anywhere right now. My arm still bled. Pain throbbed from the gunshot wound and my entire arm ached. The bullet had gone straight through, but I needed to get to a hospital. Even if I stemmed the flow of blood, I might've lost too much and though I'd essentially washed the wound with salt water, it didn't one hundred percent negate the risk of infection. Steve didn't have to find me at all. He could wait for me to bleed out.

First, I needed to stop the flow of blood from the wound somehow.

I made it into the forest and found a patch of dry

moss. The stuff was great at retaining moisture. Pressing the moss to the wound, I winced. The moss wasn't going to stay in place and holding it constantly wasn't practical either.

I cursed.

This wasn't going to work.

I set the moss down. Gripping my shirt, I tore a strip from the bottom hem. I packed the moss over the wound again and then awkwardly wrapped the fabric around my arm. Using my teeth to hold one end of the fabric, I looped the homemade bandage into a knot and pulled it tight. Tentatively, I moved my arm. Pain shot through my entire body and smacked my brain, but the bandage held in place.

Better.

And it would have to do for now. How much of my lead had I already used up?

I staggered to my feet and picked my way through the forest. With depleting energy, making it back to the cabin for a showdown with Steve seemed like less and less of a good idea with each step. I didn't need to get to the cabin.

I needed a hiding place.

Stepping over exposed roots and trees, I kept to the areas with spongy moss to reduce the sound I made as I walked through the forest in addition to concealing my tracks. Up ahead, the ground cover grew denser and harder to navigate. The trees closed in and the thick canopy overhead cut out the warm sunlight. I carefully maneuvered around the branches and twigs until I sat in the middle of a bush with broad leaves so dense, I couldn't easily peer out to the other side.

"I'll find you," Steve hollered in the distance. He sounded far off which meant he hadn't found my trail, yet, and I hadn't missed another tracker hidden in my clothes or shoes.

I leaned back, careful not to rustle the surrounding bush and stared up at the tall evergreen trees. I needed to find a way out of this, but first, I needed rest.

With thick moss surrounding me, I sank farther down, finding a more comfortable position on the uneven ground.

Death magic swirled around me.

A bone jutted out from the moss. An old bone, the power weak.

I froze.

I opened my senses and reached out. Death magic surged up, faint, but there. Pulling the moss free, I wrapped my hand around the bone and pulled. It broke free from the dirt underneath, bringing with it some ripped fabric.

A human bone.

One of Steve's victims must've crawled into this bush to die.

She would've been so alone and scared.

I hugged the bone to my chest and squeezed my eyes shut. Tears trickled out from beneath my eyelids to run down my face.

Most people would freak out from discovering human remains.

Not me.

A necromancer needed bones, blood, and power.

And now I had all three.

TWENTY-ONE

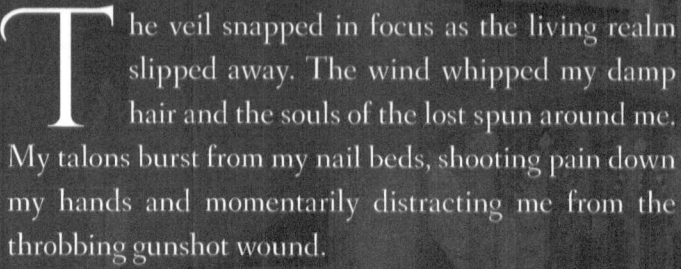

The veil snapped in focus as the living realm slipped away. The wind whipped my damp hair and the souls of the lost spun around me. My talons burst from my nail beds, shooting pain down my hands and momentarily distracting me from the throbbing gunshot wound.

"Here for our date?" a familiar deep voice spoke behind me. "You've chosen an interesting outfit."

I yipped like a small dog and spun around.

The shimmering mist rolling over the barren wasteland parted to reveal Leviathan standing outside the gates to his castle. Under a long leather jacket, he wore a white shirt tucked into leather pants. To complete the look, he had on tall leather boots.

He looked like he had planned to audition for a Dracula movie and if I were a casting director, I would've given him the part from his appearance alone.

Instinctively, I reached for my bond with Gregor again and felt nothing. The connection had faded too much.

I was stuck here with no way home.

Leviathan tilted his head and waited. He didn't know my bond had faded, and he probably still wanted to use me for something. Maybe I could get him to send me back to the living realm. Maybe I could swing this in my favour and somehow survive.

The only downside to my newly forming plan was whenever Leviathan opened portals for me, they were always to my last location, and I had no desire to return to Murder Island while Steve continued to hunt me.

"Our date?" I asked. "Of course. How would you like to start our date with a little role playing?" I held up my arm. "You could be my hot and talented doctor."

Leviathan flared his nostrils and flashed his teeth. Maybe waving my damaged, bleeding arm at a super-natural being with long fangs, unknown origins and a hankering for death magic wasn't a great idea. He might stop considering me dating material and start looking at me as a midday snack to appease his appetite.

"I happen to be very good at tending to wounds." He stepped back and waved graciously at the path leading to the front entrance of the castle. "Do you need me to carry you?"

Probably, but I couldn't bring myself to admit it. "I need you to promise me safe passage."

Leviathan sighed and clucked his tongue. "I'm hurt you feel the need to request such a thing."

I shrugged and held my breath. I really had nothing to barter with except that he really wanted me here and had no idea I couldn't pull myself back to the living realm.

"You have my word I will not seek to harm you unprovoked. I will also return you to the living realm when you wish to return."

I tried not to sigh in relief.

And failed.

I nearly fell to the ground. The blood loss had left me lightheaded.

"I know you don't have enough of Gregor's blood to anchor you with a bond. I can also deduce from your mangled arm, torn shirt and wet clothes that you found yourself in a dangerous position in the living realm and most likely travelled here to escape," Leviathan said. "A last-ditch effort at survival."

Damn. He was good.

"I will heal you and provide you with safe haven. In fact, I think I'd like to call in that favour."

I narrowed my eyes. I was already at his mercy. He'd already promised me safety and a return ticket home. Why would he waste the favour I owed him now?

He smiled, his gaze flashing.

Nothing in my research suggested the Lord of the Veil could read minds, but now I definitely suspected he had the ability.

"What is the favour you'd like to request?"

"I request you stay here, let me heal your arm, and then go on a date with me." He waggled his finger at me. "The favour is that you give me a chance. This will be a genuine date. You need to be open minded and allow yourself to get to know me."

Kang's face flashed in my mind, and I swallowed. I didn't know if I could do what Leviathan requested, but if it meant I was off the hook for owing Leviathan a favour and would solve all my immediate problems and the threat to my life, maybe I could fake it.

And Kang?

He'd want me to survive.

"Know the man, not the myth?" I said, my voice sounding hollow even to myself.

He considered me for a moment, scanning my face with that eerie dark gaze of his before answering. "Something like that."

"Well, that's something I can do." I looked over my shoulder even though it wouldn't reveal a window to the living realm. "Just so happens, I need to kill a bit of time."

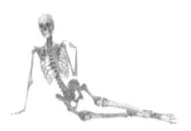

THE WROUGHT iron castle gates loomed closer and closer with each step. The pain in my arm intensified and my head spun. Something howled in the distance, the sound splintering the silence. It wasn't like a wolf howl; it was deeper and rougher and made all the hairs on my neck stand up.

"Almost there," Leviathan said.

The Lord of the Veil had offered words of encouragement. I might very well be hallucinating. Or dying.

The howling grew closer, others joined in.

Barghests.

If my limbs weren't already cold from shock, blood loss and the frigid ocean, I'd shiver at the thought.

I didn't know much about the demon dogs—only that they killed necromancers on sight and ate souls for breakfast.

The rare instances I found images of barghests online or in books, they looked like freakish werewolves, only bigger and surrounded by souls. But if no one survived an encounter with one, how could anyone draw a true depiction of the beasts?

Most likely, the artists weren't necromancers or witches. Instead, they created images from their imagination. And right now, my imagination ran wild, even though each step toward the gate sent jolting pain through my body. "Could you maybe heal me now?"

Leviathan peered down at me, the shadows of the veil playing with the hard angles of his face. "Unless you want to meet a pack of barghests, we need to cross the threshold to my castle first." He didn't seem overly concerned—about two hundred feet separated us from the gate.

Maybe he wished to avoid the barghests because I posed as a liability, and he didn't want to exert the energy required to defend me. Or maybe the barghests posed as much of a danger to him as they did to me.

Interesting.

I packed the information away in my pain addled brain and kept my mouth shut. Following Leviathan, I lurched toward the gates.

A growl snarled behind us, and I stumbled. Looking over my shoulder, I gasped.

There, perched on the top of a rock formation jutting out from the mists, stood a terrifying monster. Shaped like a wolf, only much larger, with thick black fur covering its body, the barghest had horn-like tufts poking out from its fur along the base of its skull to make it look like it had a spiky, smoky gray mane—or maybe a demonic halo. The barghest glared down at us with its glowing whitish-blue gaze.

My blood ran cold.

Green and blue death energy swirled around the barghest's massive body and when it opened its snout to snarl, revealing long, razor-sharp teeth, more death energy lit up its entire face.

The barghests in the area answered the call. They were closer now.

"Come on," Leviathan's strong voice urged me forward.

The barghest behind us roared. The deep vibration rattled the air and shook the ground beneath my feet. My still damp clothes stuck to my skin as I tried to move. My muscles screamed in protest and my lungs ached. I tripped and fell.

"We don't have time for this," Leviathan said. He ran back to me, scooped me up like a bag of dog food and flung me over his shoulder. He sprinted toward the gates.

The barghests rushed forward, sinewy muscles rippling under their sleek coats.

My heart raced. My head pounded. My arm pulsed with pain and Leviathan's shoulder punched into my stomach with each step and made me want to vomit.

The barghests were gaining on us and snapping at the dust turned up in our wake.

I held my breath as Leviathan picked up the pace, my body flailing around, my wet clothes slapping against his leather jacket. We had to make it. Had to. I refused to make it this far only to become a barghest snack.

Leviathan raced through the gates and over the threshold. As soon as his feet hit the stonework, death magic leapt from the ground and spread over the courtyard.

The howling stopped.

I released a long pent-up breath. Leviathan gently set me on my feet, his hands lingering on my bare waist. I turned to face the gates and Leviathan dropped his hands and took a step back. The barghests stood on the other side, their eerie white-blue gazes trained on me. They didn't bark, snarl, or roar. They didn't even pant or claw the dirt with their long, dark claws. They stood perfectly still in their silence as the ethereal fog rolled along to shroud them once again in shadows.

"Well." I took a deep breath. "That was awful." I looked over at Leviathan. He was breathing a little heavy and the exposed part of his white shirt was damp and dirty, thanks to my clothes, but otherwise looked like he'd just come in from a leisurely stroll on the promenade.

I stepped toward him and careened to the side. My vision wavered. I'd lost so much blood.

Leviathan caught me, his dark eyes flashing as he towered over me. "I'm going to heal you now. But I feel compelled to warn you. Healing with death magic will be uncomfortable."

"I'm already in a lot of pain." Actually, everything had started to go numb and my head grew light, which worried me the most. "How much more uncomfortable can it get?"

"It's not that kind of discomfort. At least not for a necromancer." He reached forward and ripped off the makeshift bandage. The blood soaked moss fell to the ground with a loud plop. He placed his hand over the wound and death magic flooded the air around us. His power was immense, suffocating. The magic coiled around my arm like a snake and without notice struck. Power flooded my system and dark warmth from within answered. Heat pooled low in my belly as pleasure tingled every nerve ending in my body.

I moaned and sagged into Leviathan. His strong arms caught me as his magic continued to pump into me.

"Imagine how good things would be between us," he whispered into my ear. "I can give you things. I can make you feel, truly feel. None of those drabs can make you ache the way I can."

Apparently, the discomfort was sexual and now I was really turned on.

Yet it wasn't the Lord of the Veil's face I saw when I closed my eyes and pleasure swept through me.

Nope.

I saw Connor.

I really should've kissed him.

"All done." Leviathan's deep voice grabbed my attention, and I snapped my eyes open to find myself still cradled in his arms.

I pushed away from Leviathan's rock hard body, and he dropped his arms. His magic eased away, leaving me with a feeling of emptiness.

Leviathan nodded at my healed wound. "It will still ache for a few weeks. The new skin might break and bleed. It's very thin and tender. I could do more if we exchanged blood."

Alarm bells blared in my head. I shoved my hands in my pockets. "The wound is already so much better. Thank you."

"You're welcome. I can't say that's how I imagined starting our date, but I also can't say I'm upset over it." He straightened, his dark gaze flashing. "Are you okay?"

"You could've warned me about what kind of discomfort to expect."

"And what would be the fun in that?" His lips quirked up and he waved at the path leading to the castle's entrance. "After you."

CHAPTER
TWENTY-TWO

My sneakers squeaked on the shiny obsidian floor tiles, while glowing magical orbs stuck to the ceiling illuminated the path ahead of me. The black stone walls had engravings etched into the matte surface and appeared to move as the eerie light danced off them. The inside of Leviathan's gothic-style castle looked just as intimidating as the outside. Long, dark corridors, high ceilings, old portraits in gilded frames of people long since passed and shadows around every corner.

Who were the people in the portraits? And who cleaned this place?

There wasn't a cobweb in sight. Unless the furniture came to life and mopped the floors when no one was looking, someone had to clean. Even if spiders didn't exist in the veil, dirt and dust certainly did.

I considered Leviathan's broad back and wide

shoulders as he ambled down the hallway ahead of me. I couldn't picture him with a broom and dust bin. Nor could I picture him on all fours with a scrub brush.

Maybe he had the souls do the cleaning.

We turned down another hallway, this one lined with more portraits in ornate, gold-painted frames. While I got a personal tour of a magical castle in the veil, what was happening in the living realm? Had Logan, Brandon or Kang noticed my absence yet? Maybe they had, but did they realize I'd been abducted? And what about Steve? Was he scouring Murder Island for me or was he back at his cabin with his feet up and his rifle propped nearby ready to take me out if I walked through the door?

"Who are all these people?" I waved at the portraits, deciding to ask about them instead and take my mind off thoughts of home.

"People from long ago, so long the memories of them have faded and their souls have long since moved from these lands." He flicked his hand at the next portrait we passed without pausing or hesitating.

He didn't sound like he lied, but he definitely hid something—like his words, though true, wrapped around the truth instead of revealing it.

"Okay..."

"I have lived for a long time, Lark." He glanced over his shoulder. "Sometimes memories are best to let go. Over time, they fade along with the pain."

"A long time?" What a vague statement. Did he

even know how many years had passed in the living realm?

"Yes."

"Is it safe to assume we're talking at least a few hundred years?"

He inclined his head.

"Yet, you want to date me?" I folded my arms over my chest. Yeah, I wasn't buying it. I might be a professional, I might navigate serious situations with relative ease, but no one would ever accuse me of being an old soul. Hell, Estelle hung out with me because I was the exact opposite of that.

"The dating pool in the veil is remarkably small," he said, tone dry.

I snorted and covered my mouth.

"But yes, I want to *date* you," he said. "You are an alluring individual. What better way to help me feel young and more connected with today's world than to date someone who is living it?"

Well, crap. That was almost exactly what Estelle had said.

"Are you friends with Estelle?" I asked.

He cocked his head to the side like an apex predator considering the silly behaviour of its prey. "Who?"

"Human servant."

"I don't believe so," he said. "I don't exactly get out much. Have you exchanged blood with her? I should've sensed that."

Yeah, that wasn't creepy at all.

"We don't have that kind of friendship," I said while mentally adding "blood exchange with human servant" to the list of things to research when I got out of here. Why would anyone go through a blood exchange with a human servant? Did it work similarly to that of a vampire bond? Or was it something else?

"Pity. Blood exchanges, especially with a human servant, can be highly erotic."

Oh. Well. There was my answer. Did that mean exchanging blood with anyone touched by death would have similar effects?

When I'd exchanged a small bit of blood with Gregor to form the bond, it had been uncomfortably stimulating as well. And that, along with Leviathan's comment, and our little healing session earlier, told me how exchanging blood with Leviathan would feel. It would be addicting, like a drug.

And he'd casually offered it to further heal my arm.

"Yeah, we're not going to be those kinds of friends, either." I wouldn't be that kind of friend with Leviathan, no matter how much his magic made my blood sing. It didn't take more than two brain cells to figure out how dangerous forming an intimate connection with the Lord of the Veil would be.

Leviathan shrugged and waved me into a room past heavy wooden doors. "You'd be amazed how much your opinion and feelings can change over time. Maybe one day, you'll wish to exchange blood with me. This is a date after all, and you promised to keep an open mind."

I stepped into the room after him and almost fell over.

A library.

Like one from a fairy tale.

If I ever found myself in a horror movie, I wouldn't be the asshat who got in the car with the murderer. I wouldn't forget to turn off my ringtone or ignore all the signs of a serial killer. My weakness would be books. I'd get lost in a fictional world without realizing everything around me was going to shit. They'd find me dead, hunched over a book with a knife in my back and a smile on my face.

I turned to Leviathan. "How did you know?"

"Over the last few hundred years or so, I've come to the conclusion that most women just want a quiet place to read a good book."

"Leviathan—"

"Levi."

"Leviathan—"

"Levi." He dipped his chin. "I insist."

I sighed. "I think you might be reading my mind."

He smiled, slow and wide enough to show off his long point fangs, before he waved his arm at the room for me to walk ahead of him into the space. "I have many skills, Lark, but mindreading isn't one of them."

I shook my head and walked forward a couple of steps. A dark-stained, solid oak table, at least ten feet long and five feet wide sat in the centre of the room with matching leather chairs tucked around it. The walls were lined with floor-to-ceiling bookshelves, stained the same dark colour. Every shelf was stuffed with books. For every ten feet of shelf space, there was a tall window, almost floor-to-ceiling, with a cushioned bench at the base. Fluffy pillows and soft throw blankets lay stacked in each reading nook and my fingers itched to grab the nearest book, settle in, and lose track of time.

"I think this will be an excellent first date," Levi said.

"Wh...what?"

"A reading date. It will also help settle your mind after your traumatic experience. Maybe you'll even tell me about it when you're ready. Pick a book. Pick a spot. Let's read together."

I narrowed my eyes. "You said you couldn't read my mind."

"And I can't." He smiled again, flashing his fangs yet somehow not coming across as scary as before. "But I can read body language."

Well, that wasn't very disconcerting at all.

TWENTY-THREE

I curled up on the cushioned bench with the book, wrapped in blankets and surrounded by pillows. After using a small bathroom off the side of the library to wash off the blood and sweat, I'd found a book and a spot and tried to relax. Only a few hours ago, I'd been shot and running for my life and my mind still reeled and looped through the same unanswered questions from before.

Did Steve still search for me on Murder Island, or had he given up and returned to Victoria to find his next victim? Would he try to hurt Kang? He seemed fixated on the detective. My detective.

Had anyone noticed my absence yet?

I tightened my grip on the book's hardcover, then forced myself to loosen my grip.

Logan and Brandon would be so worried. Mom, too.

And Kang? How would he feel?

My body heated, warmth flooding my cheeks. I looked away from the blurred lines in the mystery book in my hands and turned my attention to the scenery outside the window. There wasn't much to see. The veil was a barren wasteland full of shadows, mist, and lost souls. The only thing separating the castle from the ethereal mists were the surrounding curtain wall and those horrid, spiked skeletons. More bodies had joined the line-up since the last time. I wouldn't have noticed except some looked fresher. They still had flesh attached to their bones and contemporary clothing hung from their limbs.

"Ah," Levi said. He'd taken a seat on the floor to rest his back on the bench I sat on. He turned to study me without me realizing it and now he wore an unreadable expression. "You're no longer thinking about books."

"No." I'd been thinking about Kang and then tried to distract my thoughts with depressing scenery. But I couldn't tell Levi that. We were supposed to be on a date, and I promised to give him a chance and keep an open mind.

"I wish I could be confident your thoughts involved me."

I narrowed my eyes. He might not read minds, but he must have additional senses because I refused to believe he got all that from my blush. I could've just been reading a naughty scene in a book after all. I liked my books on the spicier side. Could he hear my heart-beat? My sharp intake of breath? Was that it?

"Why do you stake them?" I asked. "The bodies."

Ah yes. Classic redirect. He wouldn't see through that at all.

Levi hesitated. "They are the remains of my enemies. Staking them anchors their souls in the veil and prevents them from moving on or from being called upon by necromancers."

"I thought all souls in the veil were lost."

He pressed his lips together, probably debating how to explain it or choosing how much he wanted to share. "It's more complicated than that. If the veil only housed lost souls, you wouldn't be able to recall every soul to you, would you? All souls come to the veil, and this is where you call them from. There isn't a heaven or hell so much as the veil has many layers. The souls waiting to get reborn are all in a specific area. Some souls can move between the layers. And of course, your magic can force them to travel through the layers. But these?" He jerked his chin at the window. "Those souls will never move unless I allow it."

Okay then.

"I can smell him on you," he said.

"What?" I jerked my head back from peering out the window. I'd been wondering what the heck those people did to Levi to warrant eternal immobility. But now I wondered something else entirely. "Who?"

"Not the man who harmed you. That scent is

tangier and filled with rage. This man's scent lays beneath the latest one. It's subtle, like expensive cologne and a little smoky."

Geez.

Levi tapped his nose. "This man must've been the one you were thinking about just now. Does your heart already belong to him?" He rose to his knees and now studied me at eye level. "Or can I steal it?"

"My heart?"

"Yes. If he has a piece of it, I wish to steal it away." He leaned forward. "I wish to make you mine."

"It will take more than books."

"I have more to offer than books." His lips quirked and he raised his arm to cup my face and run his thumb over my lips. My heartbeat sped up at the promise in his gaze. Warmth flooded my body and Levi's pupils dilated. His grin widened. "Maybe, I can steal your heart after all."

He released his magic, and it curled around me to strum my skin and stir heat from within. I closed my eyes and pleasure danced along my limbs and brushed my nerves. I bit back a moan.

My eyes popped open, and I found Leviathan leaning over me. He closed the distance and pressed his deliciously full lips on mine. I expected power and intensity, what I got was gentle and seductive. He teased my lips, tasting my mouth as his magic made my body purr. Heat pooled between my legs, and I reached out to grip his shirt.

This was wrong.

Magic-induced passion...

Despite the potency of his power and how he made me feel, I didn't want the Lord of the Veil. Another man's presence flooded my mind and I gently pushed Levi away. He leaned back, his gaze smouldered with more promise. My body hummed with need to continue the kiss, to give in and let him do incredibly dirty, yet delicious things to me.

Before I could process exactly what had happened between us, a man barged into the library. With light brown hair, fair skin, and blue eyes, his familiar face jolted me out of the little fairy tale moment.

Ice clamped my spine, and I froze where I sat.

"There you are." Hudson halted in his tracks when his gaze landed on me. He wore the same thing he had on during our "date" when he tricked me into retrieving the Book of the Dead and taking him to the veil—a fitted T-shirt, jeans, and white runners.

When I'd used Gregor's bond to flee that night, I'd left Hudson behind, but he didn't look like he spent any time suffering. Or dying, for that matter.

My heart thundered while my stomach twisted in a knot. To think I spent a hot second feeling guilty for leaving this guy in the veil.

"I thought you were dead," I blurted.

"Umm..." Hudson took a step back. "I'll uh...find you later."

When I'd first met Hudson, he seemed so normal,

so mortal and different from anything else in my life. A drab. Turned out, he was far more complicated than I'd anticipated.

Levi sighed and stood up. "You may as well come in. There's no point hiding what Lark is sure to find out."

I stiffened in my seat. "Find out what?" I folded my arms over my chest. The answer was staring me right in my face. "You two were working together?" I pointed at Hudson. "You always intended to hand over the book to Levi." I pointed at my chest. "And I'm the biggest fucking chump."

Neither of these men wanted to date me.

Okay, wow. I could wallow in my personal feelings later. I knew a man who really did want to date me and even if he didn't, I didn't need or want a man's attention to justify my existence or provide me with validation.

I was a strong independent woman, dammit.

Focus, Lark.

Hudson grimaced. His gaze dropped to my hands. "Your nails..."

I shoved my hands under the blanket. I had no wish for my talons to become the main topic. I still didn't know why the talons appeared and now seeing Hudson look completely normal in the veil, I had to accept that my talons weren't a typical necromancer thing. I already suspected, but inspecting Hudson now, another necromancer, my last hopes of being a regular run-of-the-mill death raiser fled.

Hudson leaned forward. "Your eyes…"

What was wrong with my eyes?

"Beautiful, aren't they?" Levi studied my face before winking.

Apparently, he hadn't given up trying to seduce me, even though I had confirmation he wanted something other than my heart.

"I get why Levi agreed to this deal," I said, pointing my finger at Levi and then at Hudson. "Everyone covets that old book, and you had access to it, but why would you agree to work with the Lord of the Veil? You're now stuck here."

Hudson rocked back on his heels. "It got me out of the living realm. Instead of being a lackey for my brother, I can live here and become a lord of the veil."

"I highly doubt Levi will hand over his power." I glanced over at our host for confirmation.

He shrugged. "You're quite right. Hudson doesn't want to take my power, though. He merely wishes to build his own."

Maybe the veil allowed him to do that, but how would he sustain himself? He still needed food—something the veil didn't have in abundance. "How do you survive?"

Hudson shifted his weight from foot to foot and glanced at Levi.

"It's rather simple," Levi answered. "I open a

portal, send him through and then he calls one of the spirits who work for me, and they haul him back."

"And the promise of more power keeps him from running away?" I peered at Hudson. He wasn't a naïve nor ignorant guy, but for an intelligent human being he was making an awful lot of questionable choices. He had returned to the living realm, multiple times, yet willingly came back to the veil. Why?

"That and the blood bond," Levi said.

I raised my eyebrows.

"I've tasted his blood and now I can find him easily," Levi explained.

And I'd almost let him have mine.

Another thought snuck into my mind. Hudson had been back to the living realm. He'd returned and I hadn't known. I jabbed my finger in the air at Hudson. "You used your limited time on the living plane to fuck with me and leave me flowers?"

Hudson jerked back. "Why would I do that?"

I froze. That wasn't the reaction I'd expected.

Well, crap. Now what?

I'd accused almost every person in and out of my life and yet none of them had left the roses. If it wasn't the boys fucking with me, Kang, Gregor, Steve or Hudson...who was it?

"I didn't get you flowers, Lark." He frowned at me. "I go in, get supplies, and get the fuck out. I have no wish to run into my brother."

I shook my head. Hudson's brother must be a real

head case to make Hudson run to the veil and bind himself irrevocably to Levi just to get away from him. "Who's your brother?"

Hudson scowled. "You wouldn't know him. He's a real piece of work and you better hope you never cross his path. He wanted me to bring you by his coffee shop, but thankfully you said no."

Wait...coffee shop. No...No, it couldn't be...

Chills wracked my body and my heart threatened to burst free of my chest.

"My brother's name is—"

My whole body tensed as the cold crushed my chest. "Steve."

He reeled back as if I'd slapped him. "How do you know that?"

"Your brother is more than just a real piece of work."

Hudson grunted. "You have no idea."

"Oh, I think I fucking do."

Levi watched me intently, probably picking up every subtle shift in my emotions. Right now, he should be picking up a whole truckload of rage.

Hudson stilled. "What did he do to you?'

"You first."

"He had me raise an angry spirit to chase cheating women. The spirit was anchored to his coffee shop so when the angry spouses sat and watched, it would hitchhike a ride home with them, possess the men and kill the women."

"That was you?" I said. "You raised Candace MacKinnon?"

He nodded and looked away. "I had no idea that was the case you were working on when we met."

"There's something I don't get." Actually, there were several things, but I had to pick one and focus. "If you're also a necromancer, why did you bring me into this debacle? You could've come here on your own."

"I'm not like you."

"What's that supposed to mean?"

Levi interjected. "I think what he's trying to say is he's not as powerful as you."

"He was strong enough to empower a rage-filled spirit. He unleashed a murderous ghost. That's awfully powerful."

"Powerful, yes, but he didn't have the strength to raise that witch and break through her magical possession's protective barrier. Only a truly strong necromancer can touch the Book of the Dead and not be consumed with its power."

Hudson glared at Levi.

My mind drifted back to the angry spirit case. "Do you know why Steve made you do it? Why he wanted the evil spirit in the first place?"

"I told you why. The spirit would go after cheating spouses."

"Yes, I understand that part." I'd been a part of the investigation, after all. We'd made the connection between the victims by catching them on video surveillance from the club. "But...why? Why would Steve do this? Did he get cheated on in the past?"

"Ah..." Hudson looked away again. From this angle, the family resemblance was more noticeable. I should've picked up on it sooner. Steve hadn't just appeared familiar because he'd served me coffee once before. It was because he looked like his brother.

Maybe I wouldn't die in the library in a horror movie after all. Maybe I really would be the one who walked into the killer's shop and ignored all the signs.

I never claimed to be the smart one in the family.

"The why is easy enough to explain," Hudson finally answered. "Steve enjoys the hunt. He would follow the possessed men and relish the aftermath of what he caused. As you know, the men died after the spirit left them, and he'd watch that, too, from a safe distance, of course."

"He moved to hunting women himself."

"No, he didn't. He's been doing that for years. He got me to raise an angry spirit to help tide him over until the next woman." He glanced at my injured arm, his eyebrows furrowing. "Is that what he tried to do to you?"

I blanched and ignored Hudson's question. At least now I understood why Hudson wanted to get away. What was the world coming to? Suddenly, Hudson didn't look like the bad guy in my life story. Or at least not the boss-level villain.

Still a diabolical asshole. Still used me. Still

culpable in the murder of who-knew-how-many women. But he wasn't the biggest douche canoe in the lake. That honour went to Steve.

"Did you ever consider saying no?" I asked. "You're a necromancer, he isn't."

Hudson laughed, a low bitter kind of chuckle before he shook his head. "Steve was never good at taking no for an answer."

"Funny. From the way he's behaving, I would've figured he'd heard it often enough."

"He has, plenty of times. He doesn't like it, and he doesn't listen to it." He nodded at the raw scar on my arm from the bullet. "Something I can see you now know firsthand. When I first said no, he killed our cat and left it on my bed. The second time, I made sure to move away and ditch any traceable information. He found me, and my dog paid the price. I reported him to the cops or at least tried to. My girlfriend at the time was the next to go missing. He sent me pieces of her and claimed he killed her in such a way that if I ever tried to say no again, I'd go down for her murder."

Hudson pressed his lips together and looked away. This fucker had dated me knowing full well his brother might snatch me at any minute to...

"Wait...Is that why Steve picked me? Because of you? Because you took me on dates to wine and dine me and use me to raise Rose and take you on a magical fucking journey to the veil? Did he somehow spot us together and that's why he wanted you to bring me to the café?"

His grimace told me everything.

Motherfucker.

I had turned down Hudson's offer for coffee but ended up going to the café later with Kang. Steve must've been practically giddy when I walked through those doors.

"I knew I'd never truly be free of Steve unless I killed him or came here," Hudson said. "I know you think very little of me, but I could never bring myself to kill Steve, though I know he deserves it. And my plans involved you before I ever met you. You didn't deserve what I did to you, and you certainly don't deserve Steve. Nobody does."

"Your brother just made it to the top of my shit list."

Hudson flashed me a half-smile.

"You're still a piece of shit."

"We do what we can to survive." He shrugged and turned to Levi. "I came to discuss that passage. I agree with your conclusions but there's something else."

The Book of the Dead. He had to be referring to the same book I'd helped him loot from a dead witch's grave. If he couldn't hold it, did that mean he had to wear gloves to read it? Or had Levi somehow removed the protections from it?

The two men exchanged a glance.

"Are you going to share?" I asked.

Hudson snapped his mouth shut.

"Not this time." Levi stepped away from the window. "Come. Your room and our meal are still being prepared. Let me show you more of the castle and the surrounding grounds while we wait." He reached down and held out his hand.

The last thing I wanted to do was leave my toasty cocoon of blankets and pillows, abandon my book, and walk around the veil with the boogeyman from Mom's bedtime stories and a weak necromancer who betrayed my trust and was involved in countless homicides.

But I also needed information, something, anything, to help me stay safe in this place if I became trapped here.

I placed my hand in Levi's, and he helped me to my feet.

I would probably regret this.

TWENTY-FOUR

After Hudson dropped those awful knowledge bombs on me, Levi led me on a tour of stone hallways that all looked the same before bringing me to a dining room. A long stone table ran almost the entire length of the room and the last three seats at the far end had been set. Glowing magical orbs cast the room in a murky orange-tinted haze and flickering candlelight played with the shadows on the walls. Levi sat at the head of the table with me taking the seat to his right and Hudson sitting to his left.

Levi provided a meal of dehydrated and preserved food from the living realm. I'd inhaled my portion, as did Hudson. I finished my last forkful of food and dabbed at my mouth with a napkin. "Thank you for the meal."

Levi nodded and raised his glass of red wine. At least I hoped it was red wine. He opted to skip a meal of solid food and chose to drink his carbs instead. He'd probably feed off lost souls later, just as the bedtime stories claimed.

"So who exactly does all the housework and maintenance around here?" I highly doubted Levi raised a hand, and I couldn't picture Hudson running around trying to set the table while his master attempted to seduce me in the library—he'd been genuinely surprised to find me here.

"Souls can be surprisingly helpful." Levi swirled the whine in his glass. "With the right motivation, at least."

"So they just do your bidding?"

He dipped his chin.

"All of them?" Was this really what the afterlife had to offer? Dusting, scrubbing toilets and setting tables for the Lord of the Veil? If this was it, maybe I should consider vampirism after all.

Levi set his wine glass down. "How much do you know about the veil, Lark?"

"I know souls come here after they die, and I can retrieve them with my magic." I mean, I knew a little more than that, but I pretty much nailed the bulk portion of my knowledge.

Levi's lips twitched. "What do you know about the power dynamics?"

"Admittedly, not much. All I know is to stay away from you and the barghests."

"Ah...barghests." He curled his lips up. "Foul creatures. They will rip apart what I would treasure."

"Souls?"

"You."

Oh.

Hudson shifted in his seat and looked away.

"So you're saying I shouldn't go out and try to pet one?"

Levi's head snapped back as if I had physically slapped him. I hadn't, but I'd managed to shock him. "Why would you do that?"

"Because they look like animals and Lark lacks any sense of self-preservation when it comes to fluffy things..." Hudson said.

My god. He'd actually listened to my rambling on our dates. I'm not sure how I felt about that.

No, wait.

My feelings were clear.

Still fucking hated him.

Levi's lips lifted in the corner and leaned toward me. "So you like to pet dangerous things?"

If I'd still been chewing my dinner, I would've choked. "Are you honestly still trying to seduce me? You can give up the act." I waved at Hudson. "Cat's out of the bag. I know you're up to something and you need me for some reason."

"Oh, Lark." Levi took another sip of wine. "Why can't I mix business with pleasure? I wasn't lying when I said I found you alluring. Nor was I misleading you when I said there was a definite lack of options for dates in the veil." He nodded at Hudson. "This one is pretty to look at, but he's not my type and he's adamant he *doesn't swing that way*."

I bit the inside of my cheek.

"I'm not even sure I know what that means, but I'm not going to waste time pursuing someone who isn't interested." He leaned in closer and set down his wine. "You on the other hand...when my magic touches you, your whole body sings."

I pressed my thighs together and tried to ignore the instant heat rising from the memory of his death magic stroking mine.

"Just because my magic likes yours doesn't mean I like you," I said.

Levi sat back in his chair. "Of course not. But it's a start."

"I think I'm going to head back to my room now." Hudson pushed away from the table. He glanced over at me before he turned to leave. Our gazes locked and he tried to convey some sort of message to me. Or the dried food disagreed with his stomach. Hard to tell, and if it was some sort of message, I didn't catch its meaning.

"For someone who has a psychopathic murdering brother, he's rather uptight," Levi mused after Hudson left the room.

"Maybe that's why he is the way he is, but I wouldn't have used uptight to describe him."

"What would you use?"

I played with the edges of the tablecloth while I thought about Hudson. He'd been charming and gave me the impression of normalcy while remaining mysterious enough to pique my curiosity.

"I'm not sure," I admitted. "He had me fooled right up until he sliced my hand open."

Something dark flashed across Levi's gaze, and he dropped his focus to my hand where I still bore the mark from the wound. It had healed cleanly, but I'd likely have a thin scar as a memento for the rest of my life.

"I'm sorry he hurt you," Levi said.

I waved my hand in the air. "On the grand scheme of things, a papercut on my hand is the least of my complaints with Hudson."

Levi's lips twitched. "And me? What complaints do you have of me?"

I set my wine glass down and leaned in. "You tried to use my attraction to your magic against me. That's very close to coercion and I don't like it."

"I couldn't help it with the healing." He held up his hand before I could comment. "Quite literally, I couldn't have prevented you from feeling the way you did and healed you at the same time. Healing that wound was more important than your feelings, and I will not apologize for saving you from bleeding out on my doorstep."

I sat back in my seat and folded my arms over my chest.

"I fully admit to using my magic later in the library. I wanted you to feel good, but I didn't rob you of your own free will. If you knew a certain act was pleasing, would you not do it? Would you not use every skill in your arsenal to pleasure your partner?"

My cheeks heated but something in Levi's darkening gaze dared me not to look away.

"I want to pleasure you. I want you so lost in the throes of passion you can't think or breathe or do anything except scream my name."

Oh...wow.

Levi leaned in, a mischievous glint sparking in his gaze and a playful tug twitching his lips. "And I can do that with or without my magic."

I nodded, more to myself than to Levi. Not sure of how to respond, I picked up my glass and drained the rest of the wine.

Levi chuckled and pushed away from the table to stand. "Come, I'll show you to your room. It should be ready now."

I took a deep breath and frowned. Not sure I wanted Levi to take me to a room at all right now, not after this conversation.

The Lord of the Veil sighed dramatically. "I'll show you to your room where I'll leave you to have a miserable, cold night alone completely devoid of pleasure. Promise."

I snorted and stood up to join him. Little did he know, I didn't need anyone else with me to feel pleasure, but I wasn't planning on touching myself or anyone else tonight. Levi might mix business with pleasure, but I didn't. I was exhausted and still needed to process what had happened over the last twenty-four hours. Or hell, longer than that. I still didn't know how long Steve took to transport me to Murder Island.

Levi led me to a guest room with a queen-sized, four-poster bed with a fluffy, sky-blue duvet, two side tables and a view of the staked remains of his enemies.

"It's lovely," I lied.

Levi leaned down and planted a kiss on my neck, right over my pulse. A shiver ran down my body and I sucked in a breath.

"Your lies taste like honey in the air," he said. "I'll see you in the morning."

"And when is that?" I looked outside. The veil always had a dark sky, illuminated by the white and blue glow from spirits.

"Whenever we want." He left me with his cryptic answer and shut the door behind him.

I sighed and flopped on the bed. The smell of fresh laundry and something floral rose from the soft material of the duvet. I'd expected bones and dust. Nothing about this place made sense.

I rolled over and surveyed the room again. The book I'd devoured earlier in the library sat on the bedside table along with two other books that had similar covers—most likely the same genre and similar style.

A surprisingly thoughtful gesture.

And he'd probably carried out the calculated task to seduce me and weaken my resolve. I couldn't lose sight of Levi's motives. He wanted to use me. It didn't matter how nice he was or how pretty. It certainly shouldn't matter how heavenly his magic felt brushing along mine. He wanted me for my magic, and I couldn't drop my guard.

I picked up the book and stretched out on my side on top of the fluffy duvet. Adrenaline still raged through my veins and, despite knowing I should sleep, I couldn't bring myself to close my eyes in this place. Maybe the mystery book in my hands would help me drift to sleep.

I read and I read, but every time my eyelids started to close, my thoughts would race to either looking down the barrel of Steve's gun, getting shot, or Kang's expression at the end of our date right before that phone call interrupted us.

I finally gave up, dropped the book on the bedside table and rolled out of bed. I searched the room but didn't find anything under the bed or in the closet. A door off to the side led to a private bathroom with a toilet, sink and shower. A gargoyle-looking statue sat on the tiled floor next to the sink. Someone had placed fresh, nicely folded towels on the counter. I stepped into the small room and glanced at the mirror.

My reflection stared back at me and stole my breath away.

My eyes.

Instead of my normal dark blue eyes, the irises surrounding my pupil had darkened. I stepped in closer. My eyes were now black—so dark that the irises appeared the same colour as my pupils, but upon closer inspection, I couldn't tell where one ended and the other began.

Why did my eyes change colour in the veil?

I held my hands up and inspected my talons. They'd stopped growing at around one inch in length. I normally kept my nails shorter—no one likes scraping out cemetery dirt and animal blood from under their nails.

Why did I have talons?

Mom raised me to follow five rules to necromancy: Never use your own blood, never meet the Lord of the Veil, never run into a barghest, never reveal your lineage, and never take more than you need.

Did my talons and changing eye colour have something to do with why Mom made us promise never to reveal our lineage? But what did that even mean? She'd never elaborated on Rule Number Four.

As both my maternal grandparents and my paternal grandfather were reportedly strong necromancers, and Dad, too, I'd never questioned why I was so much more powerful than the average death raiser—I descended from three lines, after all. But what if

Mom had lied? Or misled? Or didn't know something about our bloodline?

I'd always suspected her rule had something to do with her side of the family because we weren't allowed to tell anyone her father had also been a necromancer. According to Mom, he kept his birth surname a secret and I always figured that meant he was hiding from someone...or something.

Dad's side descended from a strong line of necromancers from Wales, but anyone who knew the origin of my last name could figure out I was a descendent of Morcant. It wasn't a secret. But was there more to Dad's side of the family than I originally suspected? Something Mom wanted to keep hidden? My paternal grandfather had worked for Gregor, just as I did now. Maybe there was more to that than Gregor let on.

And maybe I was looking at the wrong grandparents altogether. I knew very little about my paternal grandmother and had assumed she was a drab because no one talked about her having magic. But now I wasn't so sure. What if she wasn't a drab at all?

I had so many swirling thoughts. If I survived this ordeal, I planned to sit Mom down and ask some very pointed questions and hopefully, I'd get at least a few answers.

I leaned closer to the mirror, my nose almost pressed to the surface. Something glinting off to the side under the glowing orbs caught my attention. I pulled away from the mirror and squatted down. Now face to face with the gargoyle statue, I reached forward and ran my hands along the tiled floor around its base. My fingers snagged on metal, and I pulled out a chain.

My breath caught.

I held up the chain to better catch the light and illuminate the surface of the solitary pendant hanging off the gold links.

My scalp prickled, and my hands shook. I'd recognize this pendant anywhere. I had the same one. My brother had one, too, shoved in a drawer somewhere.

And my dad had also had one.

I held the pendant up to the light while my gut twisted in a knot.

Engraved in the centre of the circular pendant was a griffin holding a skull in its beak.

The symbol of Morcant.

TWENTY-FIVE

T oo restless to read or sleep, I found myself wandering the hallways of Levi's castle. My brain was probably one more discovery away from complete meltdown.

When I found the pendant in the bathroom, my hand instantly flew to my chest, but of course, I wasn't wearing my own necklace. A memory of the chain snagging and clattering to the floor while I fought with Steve in my apartment surfaced. Either he'd left it where it fell after he rendered me unconscious or he'd taken it as a trophy like the psychopath he was.

But there was no mistaking the pendant I'd found and now wore in place of my own. Who had it belonged to? My father? Had he visited and subsequently perished in this castle? But why would he come to the veil without an anchor?

Or did the pendant belong to my grandfather? Had he come here on his own or on Gregor's orders?

Or was I thinking too deeply on this? Maybe this pendant belonged to an ancestor farther up the family tree, an ancestor I had no emotional connection with.

The only thing I knew for sure was this was the pendant of Morcant. It even had the family name engraved on the other side of the pendant just like mine.

I kept running through possibilities as I moved around the eerily quiet castle. Walking around at night, shrouded in shadows, set my teeth on edge, but also provided a sense of relief at the same time. I planned to return to the library to find something a little smuttier to read when voices stopped me. A hushed conversation echoed off the stone walls. Hudson and Levi.

Why would they bother meeting secretly at night? There wasn't exactly a crowd of people or a threat of spies during the day.

Just me.

Which meant whatever they discussed involved me or they didn't want me to know the information.

"Are you sure?" Levi growled.

"Yes," Hudson answered. "See here? This clearly means you need the blood of a powerful necromancer, but this word right here? The one right before? It means *the* necromancer. If you scan back, it refers to the blood of Morcant."

"I need the blood of a necromancer who is a descendent of Morcant."

"Exactly," Hudson said.

"I already knew that."

"There's more. See this here? Depending on how you translate this word, the meaning changes. One way to interpret this is that the blood has to be a gift."

Silence answered Hudson's proclamation.

In the meantime, I remained frozen, my heart beating so rapidly, so hard, I worried it would give me away. I was a descendant of Morcant. This wasn't a coincidence. And I'd nearly given Levi my blood earlier to finish healing me.

"She has to be willing," Hudson continued. "That's the piece you were missing. That's why it didn't work before."

Before?

Levi grunted.

My hand flew to the pendant I'd tucked into my shirt.

Before.

Guess I didn't have to wonder about the fate of my family member who previously wore this pendant—I just needed to figure out which family member Hudson referred to.

"She'll never do it," Hudson said. "I don't know much, but I know that."

"Why don't we ask her ourselves?" Levi said. He raised his voice. "What do you say, Lark?"

I stiffened. No running away now. Levi had already detected my presence.

With a deep sigh, I walked over to the doorway to the library and stepped inside. "It was my racing heartbeat, wasn't it?"

Levi dipped his head. "Among other things."

I scowled. Not much I could say to that. At least nothing that would help me leave this place. "So what devious plans are you attempting to concoct?"

"I'd like to form a portal to the living realm."

"You can already do that."

He shook his head. "I can form a gate for you to leave the veil and return you to your previous location in the living realm. I can't open one for you to come here if you're on the other side, nor can I travel through the portals. Nor can I pick a location."

That was probably for the best. I clamped my mouth shut and bit down on my snarky response.

"And you need my blood?" I asked.

"Yes."

"Freely given?" I asked.

"Yes," he answered.

"Does this have anything to do with why I grow talons and my eyes turn black in the veil?"

His smile slowly spread across his face. "No. That's just an added bonus."

"Do you know why this happens to me?"

"I have my suspicions."

"Will you tell me?" I asked.

"Will you help me?" he countered.

No, I wouldn't. Though I desperately wanted to know why I got these special features in the veil, I didn't want to know so badly I'd abandon all caution.

"No," I said, out loud this time.

"Well, then...you have my answer."

"What's the catch?" I asked. "With the blood. You need it, but how much? Does it need to be a full sacrifice? Or do you only need a drop? Why didn't you just ask for my blood as your favour? Would you see me chained to your dungeon to bring me out every time you want to go on vacation? Why would you want to go to the living realm anyway? It's full of assholes like Steve and Hudson. Have you been paying attention? Our realm is a mess."

"Will you help me?" Levi asked while avoiding all my questions. Not a good sign.

"No. Definitely not right now. I need to read all the fine print and there needs to be set boundaries and responsibilities and even then, even then, I'd hesitate."

"Why?"

"Because you're the biggest, baddest, scariest boogeyman to necromancers. That's not based on nothing. I'm not going to help set you loose on the living realm." And he pretended to like me to get something from me. Just like Hudson.

And just like with Hudson, I'd fallen for it.

Motherfuckers.

I was pissed.

And my ego needed a reality check.

Levi grunted and looked away from my death stare. "One day, Lark. You'll see things my way."

Boy, did I hope he was wrong.

CHAPTER
TWENTY-SIX

I stalked back to my assigned room unsure of whether I wanted to break something or just cry. It always amazed me how closely tied those two emotions were. I considered myself a strong independent woman. But sometimes a good angry cry helped reset my focus.

Crying didn't make me weak.

And right now, I really needed to focus.

Levi swore I had safe passage and that he'd return me to the living realm when the time came. He wouldn't kill me, and he wouldn't harm me, not if he wanted my willing participation.

It was also in his best interest to keep me alive and content. Hence why he tried to seduce me.

A boot scraped the stone tile around the corner.

I froze.

I'd left Levi and Hudson to their plotting in the

library behind me. Unless one of them could teleport—something I wouldn't put past Levi—someone else was in the castle.

The little hairs on the back of my neck stood up. The air turned cold and burned my lungs. One second, I stood poised to bolt and the next, I was slammed against the wall. Pain shot down my back.

A vampire clutched my neck with one hand and held me in place. With one twitch, he could snap my neck like a twig or tear it out.

I didn't know this vampire. He had reddish brown hair and hazel eyes the colour of melted honey. He might've been handsome, but he made it difficult for me to appreciate his stone-like beauty while partially strangling me and snapping his teeth in my face.

"If he didn't warn us to leave you alone, bone witch, you'd already be dead," he snarled.

This vampire belonged to Gregor.

Thank god.

Gregor wanted me alive and maybe this guy had an alternate route home that wouldn't involve dangerous proximity to Steve's Murder Island and favourite hunting rifle.

"I need your help," I wheezed, his palm still pressing on my neck. "I need to get home."

He narrowed his eyes. "I don't give a shit what you need. You're going to tell me where it is."

"Where what is?"

"The book," he hissed. "I can sense its presence nearby. It's in this section."

"I don't—"

He squeezed my neck.

I thrashed in his hold. He may as well have been granite—he didn't budge, and his hand hurt my neck.

He eased the pressure right when I thought my head would explode and I sputtered, gasping for breath.

"Now, you're going to help me."

Sure, I knew where the book was. I'd left Levi and Hudson huddled together in the library analyzing the wording that very possibly condemned me to death or eternal servitude. But I wouldn't tell this vampire that information. I gathered my power. I might not trust Levi. He might even be my enemy, but the Book of the Dead was safer here. Under no circumstances could I allow the vampires to get a hold of it.

My magic pooled around me. Necromancy worked differently in the veil. I needed bones, blood, and power to access the veil while in the living realm, but once here, I had no such requirements.

Before the vampire demanded more answers I didn't have or crushed my throat, I thrust my magic into his body and whispered an incantation. He stiffened and slackened his grip on my neck.

I planted both my hands on his chest and pushed him back, slamming the full brunt of my magic into him as well. He staggered but held his ground. That was fine. I didn't need him to move. His honey gaze grew distant as my magic took hold.

He remained as still as a corpse.

"You will never attack me again. Do you understand?"

"Yes," he hissed. His body twitched. Was he aware of the control I had over him? Did he try to fight it?

I could never let him go. If Gregor found out I controlled vampires like corpses, he'd send his whole legion of vampires after me. It would be a slaughter. My slaughter. There was no way I could control that many.

The vampire's body jerked again.

I frowned. I hadn't told him to move and didn't feel his energy pull free of my magic. I stared down at his chest. It took a second for my brain to register the pointy end of a sword protruding from his body, an inch shy of puncturing me.

The vampire's gaze locked on mine. "When he finds out, you're dead."

I swallowed. Gregor couldn't possibly find out about what just happened unless I told him, and I didn't plan to say anything to anyone anytime soon.

"I know I said you'd see things my way given time..." Levi yanked the blade from the vampire's body and my nameless attacker toppled to the ground. "But I didn't think you'd turn your opinion around quite this fast."

"He was after the book."

271

Levi looked down at the prone body. "Was he now?"

"I'm still unsure what you're up to, but the book is safer in your care. The vampires would see humans enslaved to them as a food source."

"Maybe." He tapped his chin. "Maybe not. It's an interesting topic to discuss but not nearly as interesting as what happened here. I'd like to have a little chat about how you controlled a three-hundred-year-old vampire assassin."

"You were watching?"

He nodded.

"The entire time?"

His smile was answer enough.

"You bastard. He could've killed me."

"Ah, but if I stepped in prematurely, I never would've seen what happened next."

"It couldn't have been that exciting."

"I disagree. I learned you won't try to steal the book from me or help someone else do it, and I also discovered you're powerful enough to control vampires." His gaze dropped to my hands. "You're not just a descendent of Morcant, are you?"

I clamped my mouth shut.

"You can keep your secrets for now, but you were never in any real danger. I gave my word ensuring your safety and I take oaths made in the veil very seriously."

"I'm not sure which of those things I should be most concerned about, but I'd also like to know why you were close enough to witness everything but never said anything to me. Were you following me?"

"Of course, I was following you. I wanted to see what you'd do and whether you could sense the book while I had Harrison take it to another location."

He must've moved it from the library to see if I followed the trail. I hadn't noticed at all, but I also hadn't been trying to sense or track the book. I pushed my magic out, coating the walls and floor as it moved through the castle. Bones called out to me. Everywhere. So many bones. So many human lives...

But I'd held the Book of the Dead in my hands, and I knew the flavour of its magic.

There.

The book had been moved to a room down the hall. I let my magic fall away and kept my face impassive. I might have the power to find the book, but I had no intentions of going after it.

"Well," I said. "Now that you know you don't have to hide the silver from me, I'm going to say goodnight and find my room."

Levi scoffed and shook his head "It's more morning now and that wasn't the only reason I was following you."

"What was the other reason?"

He opened his fist to reveal a wavering soul. "It's time to send you home."

I blinked at the Lord of the Veil while the vampire assassin continued to bleed out by our feet. Levi had stabbed him through the heart, there was no coming back from that. As soon as the blood left his system, the vampire would start to rapidly decompose.

"You're sending me back? Now?"

"Yes," he said. "You have fulfilled your favour and your wound is healed. For the record, I didn't use the favour to ask for your blood because that doesn't exactly fit the requirement of freely given, does it?"

"So you opted for seduction?"

He dipped his head. "I must admit, it wasn't a hard decision to make. I want you with or without the blood and still would've tried to make you mine. I may not be happy with how things played out between us, but I hope you'll see things my way eventually. I still want you as a queen by my side."

As much as I'd look badass with a crown, the whole idea seemed terribly wrong to me.

"You have held up your end of the deal," Levi continued. "Now it's time for me to do the same."

Unease swirled in my belly. We hadn't bargained for how much time I'd spend here. "I was hoping to wait longer so Steve would assume I died."

Levi glanced at the soul quivering in his palm. It didn't zoom off so Levi must be holding it in place with his power. He most likely used the souls as informants —his own personal army of spies. What had this one told him?

"Do you trust me?" Levi asked.

No. Not at all.

I hesitated.

Levi chuckled and shook his head. "Of course, you don't."

Really, what did he expect?

"You can trust me on this." He studied the soul again and closed his hand around it. "You are safe to return. You have my word."

"Okay..." I stared at his now closed hand. Obviously, the soul had told him something significant, but what?

"Do you need to retrieve anything from your room?"

"No." I came with the clothes on my back, and I'd take the family necklace I'd found with me.

Levi nodded and waved his hand in front of us. A portal rippled through the air and formed a few feet away from me.

The section of bushes I'd hid in with the remains crystallized into view with the morning light from the rising sun.

I took a deep breath and stepped forward.

"One more thing," Levi said.

I stopped and glanced over my shoulder.

"Say hi to Connor for me."

I frowned and hesitated again. Why would Leviathan know Kang's name? And more importantly, how did he know about my connection with the detective? Had Hudson told him, or was it the soul spies? Or had Levi figured out the information some other way?

The possibilities sent bolts of unease along my skin. I had so many unanswered questions. Still.

"Time to go," Levi said. "I can't hold this open forever."

"Thank you," I said, and meant it. No matter how I felt about Levi and no matter what his ulterior motives were—and he definitely had some—he'd saved my life.

I stepped through the portal. As it closed behind me, Levi's response came through. "You're welcome."

TWENTY-SEVEN

T he thick bushes surrounded me as I stood in my hiding place. My heart thundered so loudly, it took a while for me to hear the wind through the surrounding trees and the distant cry of seagulls. Dark death energy wound around me, tantalizing, and delicious.

Like a siren's call, the magic tightened its hold on me, pulling me forward. I stumbled out of the dense bush and followed the delectable taste of death magic in the air. My sneakers sunk into blood-soaked moss, and I stopped in my tracks to mentally process the scene in front of me.

Severed body parts lay strewn across the forest floor. Tissues, organs, and a body's worth of blood painted the trampled grass, moss, and tree trunks. Blood dripped down the rough bark.

In the centre of the carnage, Connor Kang stood

completely naked except for the layer of blood coating his skin. The sunlight glinted off a gold chain wrapped around his wrist several times. My missing necklace.

Kang's shoulders heaved as he panted. Muscles tense, teeth clenched and bared, rage flashed across his expression. His eyes had darkened, appearing as if they were entirely black. The veins near his eyes looked like they pumped black blood through his body, and any skin not covered in blood had a grayish tinge that appeared to lighten as I studied him. He looked positively feral.

And like an enraptured moth attracted to a burning flame, I stepped forward, drawn to him and the power radiating off his sculpted body in waves.

Death magic.

A thousand times more alluring than Levi's, the power surrounded me, caressed my skin and sunk in to find a part of me I never showed anyone. His magic teased my mind and pleasure flooded my body.

Kang snapped his head up and his dark gaze met mine.

My breath caught in my lungs.

"How did you find me?" I asked.

Kang shook his head and closed his eyes. Some of the tension left his body. When he opened his eyes again, the black had cleared, leaving his normal brown colour. His skin also faded, slowly returning to its normal pale, but healthy pallor.

"Did you torture the assassin you have in custody?"

I asked, still moving closer, still drawn to the seductive tug of his power. "Did you use my necklace in a tracking spell?"

He kept his attention trained on me while he slowed his breathing and regained his humanity.

"How did you find me?" I asked again.

"I *am* a detective," he said, finally. His voice came out like a deep crackling growl. He stepped over Steve's decapitated head to close the distance between us. "I thought I was too late."

Before I could respond, he had me in his arms. His mouth crashed down on mine. At first, it was a hard claiming kiss as if he wanted to confirm I truly lived, as if he wasn't sure I'd somehow slip away like an apparition. Then, he turned his kiss into fire, to sear his name on my soul. And all I could do was hold on to his blood-spattered body and get lost in his touch.

I didn't think about Steve's bloody body parts strewn all around us. Nor did I worry about Levi, Hudson, the veil, or the mysterious roses that stopped appearing after I freaked out about them. I didn't think about Cathy or Lily's stolen remains, and I certainly didn't think about the weird summoning circle slaughter that remained unsolved. All thoughts and worries fled my mind, leaving only Connor.

His magic caressed mine, like a lover running fingertips over naked skin. I gasped into his mouth, and he swallowed the sound, deepening the kiss. His magic continued to press into me.

I'd been wrong. He didn't kiss like he danced. This was something else. Better. More.

My body hummed with anticipation and need. I wrapped my arms around him, ignored the carnage around us, and kissed him back. If he etched his name on my soul, then I'd do the same.

My magic wrapped around his, holding tight while sliding deliciously along the bands of power. Connor growled against my lips, the deep rumble vibrating my chest. If we didn't stop soon, I'd end up throwing him down in Steve's bloody remains and riding Connor into oblivion.

Connor groaned and pulled away. His gaze flashed and his hands tightened on my waist. I understood what he said without speaking. I didn't want him to let go, either.

The death magic I'd sensed earlier receded, called back and contained behind whatever shield Connor used to hide his true nature. Only a whisper of his magic remained.

"What are you?" I asked.

Kang's expression turned grim, but he kept his flashing gaze focused on me when he answered. "I'm a barghest."

~Thank you for reading~

Lark Morgan's
Rules to Necromancy

1. ~~Never use your own blood~~

2. ~~Never meet the Lord of the Veil~~

3. ~~Never run into a barghest~~

4. Never reveal your lineage

5. Never take more than you need

CHARACTERS

Amelia Mills: second victim

Amy Steele: first victim

Bernice "Bernie" Olsen: Maggie's previous owner

Brandon Callahan: Logan's boyfriend

Candace MacKinnon: evil murderous ghost

Connor Kang: detective with the Victoria Police Department

Denise Ray: Lark's friend, co-worker, and fellow necromancer

Drabs: non-magical, non-supernatural humans

Estelle Beaumont: French. Gregor's human servant

Glamies: supernatural beings. Named after their ability to "glamour" even though many glamies cannot use glamour. Glamy (sing.)

Grant Malone: club owner of Spiral

Gregor Fissore: Italian. Master vampire of Victoria

Hudson Harrison: former client

Oliver Jacobs: detective with the Victoria Police Department

Leviathan: Lord of the Veil

Lily Zheng: ghost. Chinese name: Zheng Mei Hua

Logan Morgan: assassin, Lark's twin brother

Lark Morgan: necromancer, Logan's twin sister

Maggie: so much more than just a cat

Odette Mills: Amelia's sister and roommate

Officer Daniels: VicPD officer

Officer Rodriguez: VicPD officer

Peter Schmidt: court appointed adjudicator for estate disputes

Pierre Deveau: vampire

Spiral: popular club downtown

Steve: barista

Timothy Richards: potential summoning circle victim

ACKNOWLEDGMENTS

It truly takes a team of wonderful, and patient, people to create a story and make it ready for publication. I'd like to thank my friend Cindy Cheung for helping me appropriately select a Chinese name for Lily Zheng; Nicole, Wendy and Karen for beta reading; Lara Parker for editing; Book Nook Nuts for proofreading; Tricia Beninato for the gorgeous cover, and my friends and family for putting up with me. I can't thank everyone enough for their support, assistance and words of encouragement.

And most of all, I'd like to thank you, the reader, for continuing to support me.

J.C. MCKENZIE

I'll break all the rules...

Life as a necromancer is never easy, but when the body of a ghost from my past turns up, inexplicably whole, very dead, and without a soul, I seriously reconsider my chosen profession. What good am I as a necromancer if I can't raise the dead?

I might be a failure, but I'm still in high demand. The vampires want me to raise their progeny. The Lord of the Veil wants me to help him escape the veil. The police want me to continue solving their murder cases without giving me a pension.

And Detective Connor Kang wants me, too. Just me.

He makes the magic in my blood sing and now I know his true identity and what's in his heart. But as it turns out, Kang isn't the only person in my life harbouring a secret.

I need to rescue a supernatural hostage, figure out who or what is capable of destroying souls, and somehow stay alive and out of the clutches of those who would seek to kill or use me. Mom raised me to follow five sacred rules to necromancy, and I've faithfully followed every single one.

Until now.

A deliciously dark Urban Fantasy tale with a flawed necromancer trying to survive a harsh supernatural world by International Bestselling Author, J. C. McKenzie.

Purchase *Death Taker* today!

Https://books2read.com/DeathTaker

Warning:
the spice increases in this last instalment
of the Lark Morgan trilogy.

ABOUT THE AUTHOR

J. C. McKenzie is a book loving, gumboot-wearing, unapologetic science geek. She predominantly writes urban fantasy and post-apocalyptic dystopian fantasy with strong romantic elements. When she's not spinning tales, she's in the classroom sharing her passion for science and mathematics while secretly warping the young, impressionable minds of our future to carry out her evil plans for world domination. She lives in the Pacific Northwest with her family.

Visit her at jcmckenzie.ca

facebook.com/j.c.mckenzie.author

x.com/JC_McKenzie

instagram.com/j.c.mckenzie

tiktok.com/@jcmckenzie0

bookbub.com/authors/j-c-mckenzie